MW01610704

Husbands and Lap Dogs
Breathe Their Last
A Cummings Flynn Wanamaker Mystery

by

David Steven Rappoport

Mainly Murder Press, LLC
PO Box 290586
Wethersfield, CT 06129-0586
www.mainlymurderpress.com

Mainly Murder Press

Editor: Judith K. Ivie
Cover Designer: Karen A. Phillips

All rights reserved

Copyright 2016 by David Steven Rappoport

Paperback ISBN 978-0-9861780-3-0
Ebook ISBN 978-0-9861780-4-7

Published in the United States of America by

Mainly Murder Press, LLC
PO Box 290586
Wethersfield, CT 06129-0586
www.MainlyMurderPress.com

Dedication

*To my husband, Tim Tucker, who is kind, dependable,
and the only man I know who conducts
volumetric analyses of birthday cake*

~

Acknowledgments

Thanks to Donald Laventhall for his generous assistance
and to the following people who have been very helpful to
the development of this book or to my progress as a
mystery writer: Laurie Bernstein, Dan Duffy, Keith Green,
Michael Klein, Jeff Kliment, Paul Rivenberg, Rebecca
Robinson, Howard Solomon, Jennifer Stevenson, Todd
Young, and Wendell Wyatt. Thanks to Marie Gross for the
legal advice. I'd also like to thank the primary members of
my Nordic study group for their support: Christopher Dork,
Kate Early, and Rowan Hendrix.

Finally, for offering inspiration, I'd like to acknowledge
The Owen Society for Hermetic and Spiritual
Enlightenment, information about which can be found at
www.facebook.com/groups/365219873490214.

~

Then flash'd the living lightning from her eyes,
And screams of horror rend th' affrighted skies.
Not louder shrieks to pitying Heav'n are cast,
When husbands or when lap-dogs breathe their last...

Alexander Pope, *The Rape of the Lock*

~

One

Mainers take care of what they own; the weather and Yankee frugality demand it. When winter comes, they put their boats in dry dock and often shrink-wrap them in white plastic. When summer approaches, they rip the shrink-wrap off and put them back in the water.

It was early June in the village of Horeb, Maine, population 2,421, a village on Merrymeeting Bay. The weather had finally turned warm, and Elektra Philemon, with the assistance of three local boys, was about to launch her employer's boat for the season. It was stored at a neighbor's place — Ernestine Cutter's. Ernestine knew that in recent years the dock and storage fees at the town marina had become too much for Deuteronomy Smelt, the man for whom Elektra worked as a housekeeper.

Elektra was a monumental woman in late middle age, part Praxiteles and part Bride of Frankenstein, with more curves than a Greek island and a headful of frantic gray ringlets. She strode forcefully in her L.L. Bean waterproof boots across the acres of garden, septic system and muddy meadow that separated Ernestine's Greek Revival home from the bay. The leach field was particularly soft; major repairs had been done in the fall and covered over with earth just before winter set in.

As Elektra and her helpers approached, they noticed an increasingly foul smell. By the time they reached the boat, the smell was overwhelming. The shrink-wrapping, while still more or less intact around the sides of the boat, had a large gash on the surface.

"A fisher cat must have crawled in there and died," one of the boys suggested, referring to a nasty species of local weasel.

Elektra sighed and nodded in agreement. "Boys, we rip the plastic, then back to the house for bleach I going, and the boat we scrub."

Vigorously, she began to rend the white plastic that covered the boat like a cocoon. The boys assisted.

The cause of the smell was not immediately evident, so Elektra hoisted herself into the boat and looked inside the interior. Entering the front cabin, she shrieked monumentally. She climbed down to terra firma and fell to her knees, shaking her fists.

"What is it?" one of the boys asked.

She wailed. Startled by her behavior, the boys expressed fear in its more subdued Yankee form: they stood frozen. Then one of the boys, returning more quickly than his peers to his normal state of New England pragmatism, went on board to see what the problem was.

"So, is it a fisher cat?" one of his friends asked.

"No. It's a person."

The second boy joined the first in the boat. "Who is that?" he asked, peering at the remains.

"Don't know, but he looks wicked dead," the first boy said.

"Somebody should call Officer Bernier," a third boy concluded, referring to the Sagadahoc County Sheriff who lived in the village. This boy pulled a cell phone out of his pocket.

Elektra wailed again, then added, "Ask police if bringing some bleach!"

Two

Cummings Flynn Wanamaker was the result of five centuries of cynics, rabbis, radicals and unclassifiable odd balls from unremarkable portions of Eastern Europe. The family name, Wachinsky, had been changed at Ellis Island.

Cummings had dark brown hair and eyes, stood 5'8", but only when he was really trying, and had a tendency toward ovoid pudginess, which had become more and more difficult to control as the years passed. Like most short, chubby people, he longed to be tall and thin, or at least young, short and less chubby. His IQ was high, very high, but not so high as to result in actual genius. He was pleased with the wisdom that living to the age of fifty had afforded him; he often thought that if he could repackage his current knowledge in his twenty-year-old body, life would be optimal.

Cummings had a craving for the certainty of perfection. Outside of his detective work, an arena in which he was able to channel this tendency into discernment, he rarely seemed to be able to identify the perfect choice in a set of possibilities.

Some years earlier he'd implemented a reasonably effective workaround. He set the timer on his wristwatch for thirty minutes, during which he allowed himself to consider all options. Then he willed himself to make a selection or, failing that, a choice at random.

Earlier in the day Cummings had spent two hours on the Internet searching for unusual cocktails. When he had reduced the list to twenty-seven possibilities, he set the timer. Thirty minutes later, when a buzzer sounded, he was no closer to a decision. He closed his eyes and pointed at random to make a selection.

Now Cummings and his husband, Odin, along with their neighbors and best friends, Luther and Rockland, sat in Odin's and Cummings's Chicago living room, sipping the selected drink, a flaming concoction called The Burning Witch of Aragon.

The house was a bungalow, an Arts and Crafts cottage built in 1916, one of thousands of similar homes that fill Chicago's neighborhoods. On the first floor there was a tiny living room, tiny dining room, two small bedrooms (one of which was Odin's office and one of which was Cummings's) and a cramped kitchen.

Although the house was more suitable for dolls than people, it was charming. The first floor was embellished with stained glass, oak moldings and built-in oak cabinets. A friend of Odin's who, unlike Odin and Cummings, had a talent for such things had decorated it using Mission colors and furniture. The second floor was even tinier than the first, little more than a half-story, with two small bedrooms and two smaller closets; but again the decor had transformed it into a domestic museum of World War I-era taste. Cummings liked the house but thought it was good that their social life was mostly limited to at-homes with Luther and Rockland; there wasn't room for more.

"What's in this drink?" Rockland Yellowhair asked. He was of mixed American Indian and Nordic ancestry, with decidedly jet-black hair and blue eyes. He was in very late middle age and a bit like Fred Astaire—not truly handsome but tall, thin and elegant. He was rather formal and always seemed overdressed, even when he was wearing jeans and a button-down shirt, as he was presently.

"Sangria, vodka and a dash of hot sauce," Cummings explained, blowing out the flame and taking a sip. "The recipe is from a bar in Madrid called Savonarola. Apparently, it has an Inquisition theme. They serve this drink with an appetizer called *auto da fe-jitas*."

"I cannot remember when I have tasted something so inflammatory," Luther drawled languidly. He was a tall, thin, ethereal young man in his thirties with a delicate coffee-colored complexion and a neat Fade haircut that accentuated his tightly curled black hair. He was as southern as pecan pie, poisonous snakes and relatives hidden in the attic. Unlike Rockland, who only seemed to be overdressed, Luther usually was. Today he wore a white linen suit, a blue cotton shirt, a madras bow tie, wingtip shoes and a straw hat.

"You know, you needn't try so hard to impress," Rockland said to Cummings, referring to the drink. "It's only us."

"Cummings likes to entertain," Odin said in husbandly defense. He was also of Nordic ancestry and was slim, tall and blond. He was in his mid-forties, had a goatee, and wore jeans and, as always, his prized University of Illinois baseball cap.

"I don't mind the effort," Cummings replied, "though I did have some trouble narrowing the drink list."

"Let me know when you're ready for a referral for your obsessive compulsive disorder. I may have retired from medicine, but I still have a Rolodex," Rockland said.

"I don't have OCD," Cummings protested. "It's just that I sometimes have trouble sorting through options."

Cummings was fairly new to Chicago. After much of a lifetime in Manhattan, he had moved to the village of Horeb, Maine, population 2,600. He'd gone there following clues to the murder of his late partner, Terry. After several years this murder and quite a few others had been solved, and Maine's rurality had begun to seem oppressive rather than peaceful.

Cummings was thinking about moving on when he met Odin by chance while visiting Chicago. Cummings had been immediately attracted to Odin physically but even more intrigued by the fact that when he first saw him, Odin was making strange numeric doodles on a napkin.

"Are you doing your taxes?" Cummings asked him.

"No," Odin responded.

"Are you a mathematician?" Cummings tried again.

"No. I'm a computer geek, but I love math. It's one of the few areas of life where there's almost always an answer. I thought I'd just have a beer and double-check my figures."

"I see. Do you mind if I ask what you're calculating?"

"Not at all. I'm working out how many dates I have to go on to get to Mister Right."

"Can you calculate that?" Cummings asked.

"Well, you have to make some assumptions."

"Such as?"

"Conceptually, it's similar to socks in a drawer. Let's say you have forty socks, all mixed up, half of which are black and half of which are white. In order to be sure you have a pair that matches, what's the largest number you might have to pull out?"

"Twenty-one."

"Correct. My challenge is to calculate the minimum number of socks I have to pull out of the drawer, metaphorically speaking, to be likely to get to a match. Are you really interested in this?"

"Yes. Please continue," Cummings replied.

"The drawer is Cook County. The initial set of socks is the male population. According to the 2000 census, that's 2,603,532. No one really knows what percentage of the population is gay and lesbian, but I'm using four percent, which is what the British government estimates. That works out to 104,141 gay men, of whom 29,159 are in my target age group, thirty-five to fifty-four.

"The next question is, how many gay men are single? No one knows that either, but I found a large health-related survey in California in which twenty-five percent of gay men reported they were partnered. So, I'm going with seventy-five percent single. That drops the pool to 21,869. Next, I'm assuming that my matching sock has at least a bachelor's degree and is a registered Democrat. Similar education and values are important, don't you agree?"

"Yes, I do."

"That drops the pool to 4,301. At this point, things become trickier. In order to get down to anything like a manageable number of dates, I need to come up with other criteria that are quantifiable and will predict compatibility. Otherwise, to adequately sample my 4,300 guys, I'd have to go on something like 525 dates."

"So, what did you select?"

"Just one question: What do you really want in life?"

"Why did you pick that?"

"Because my last partner didn't know, and I think that's what ultimately did us in."

"That's not always easy to know," Cummings said. "What you think is fulfilling can disappear, and then you're left feeling like you're starting all over from the beginning."

"Is that what happened to you?" Odin asked.

"More or less. My partner was killed a few years ago. Murdered."

"I'm very sorry to hear that," Odin replied.

"Thank you. And what about you?"

"Do you mean, why am I single? My ex left me for an interior designer we met on vacation in Madrid."

"So, what percentage of men know what they want?" Cummings asked.

"Anecdotally, based on my first hundred dates, I'd estimate twenty-five percent."

"That few?"

"I'm afraid so. Anyway, that brings my sample down to 1,075. With a confidence of ninety-five percent plus or minus four percent, I still have to go out with around 385 men to sample the socks in the drawer."

"How many socks have you sampled so far?"

"275."

Within a few minutes Cummings became datum 276. Within a few days it seemed clear to both of them that Cummings was the study end point, even though he'd appeared earlier than projected. They began dating long distance. Eighteen months later Cummings had moved to the Windy City. That was several months ago.

"How's work, Odin?" Luther said, tactfully changing the subject as he always did when Rockland's assessment of Cummings's compulsiveness came up. "Did I not read that Multiverse Air had a substantial first quarter loss?"

"Yes, you did, though I don't see how that makes it different from virtually every other corporation on earth," Odin responded. Times were indeed tough. "They're threatening layoffs. I think we're safe in IT, though."

"I believe everybody I know is worried about their jobs," Luther said, "except Rockland, of course, as he's retired."

Rockland smiled.

"Are you worried about your job, Luther?" Cummings asked Luther.

"The music department is threatening cutbacks. Still, I have a backup plan. I believe I have mentioned my brother-in-law, Billy Goat Bates, who owns a Christian car wash in Tuscaloosa, Alabama? He has purchased a Hammond organ secondhand from a Pentecostal church that went into decline after the entire congregation died from snakebites. He would like me to play hymns for his customers while their vehicles are washed in the blood of the lamb, so to speak."

Everyone laughed.

"And you, Cummings?" Luther asked with a wry smile. "I understand congratulations are in order."

"For what? Consulting is tough right now. I hardly have any work."

"I don't mean that," Luther responded, taking a neatly folded newspaper clipping from his coat pocket. It was an article from the previous day's *Chicago Tribune*.

"'Another notable amateur Chicago sleuth is Cummings Flynn Wanamaker,'" Luther read, "'who helped the Joliet police solve a rash of murders there.'"

"I don't know how they found out about that," Cummings said modestly.

"Your business is struggling because you're in the wrong business," Rockland stated. "You should stop wasting your time working for charitable foundations and become a licensed detective."

"I've been getting calls, a few yesterday and three or four since this morning," Cummings said.

"Calls from whom?" Luther asked.

"People who read the article and looked up my number. They're looking for help solving mysteries."

"Well, there you are," Rockland said emphatically, "and if you get any juicy cases, give me a jingle. I'm busy with my musicology research but can certainly give a toxicology consult for the odd poisoning."

"Thanks, Rockland. I'm still grateful to you and Luther for your help on the Joliet case. Maybe I should give becoming an investigator more thought," said Cummings. "I'll look into it."

"You do that," Rockland replied.

"I think we should get a move on," interrupted Odin, "or we'll be late for our reservation."

After dinner, as they were walking back to the car, Luther pulled Cummings aside.

"Do you have plans tomorrow?"

"Not really," Cummings replied.

"I have been invited to a meeting of the Mathers Society."

"What's that?"

"I do not know exactly, but it has something to do with the occult. Of course, I would never invite Rockland or Odin. They are just too left-brained, but I thought you might like to accompany me."

"You don't think I'm left-brained?" Cummings asked, mildly offended.

"Not like they are. I think of you as more open-minded on dubious matters."

"Perhaps. Still, why would we want to go to the meeting of an occult group?" Cummings responded.

"Because it is something entirely different. Also, I feel it is politic to make an appearance, as the invitation came from Anunciación Hollingberry."

"Who is Anunciación Hollingberry?"

"One of the benefactresses of the music department and a delightful, if slightly unusual, lady I consider to be a personal friend."

"Unusual? In what way?" Cummings asked, intrigued.

"Several ways," Luther said teasingly, "but you will have to accompany me to experience her idiosyncrasies."

"Okay," Cummings said. "What time will you pick me up?"

Mid-morning the following day, Luther appeared at Cummings's door wearing an Edwardian morning suit, complete with top hat and cane.

"Ready to go?" Luther asked Cummings.

"You didn't say it was a costume party."

"Did I not mention that Anunciación said that Steampunk dress was preferred?"

"What on earth is Steampunk?"

"As I understand it, it started as a genre of science fiction in which nineteenth-century technology, particularly steam power, was reimagined in a fantasy world of the future. I believe the movement has now gone far beyond literature. There are Steampunk conventions and Steampunk music and Steampunk crafts and heaven knows what. Late Victorian and Edwardian clothing with certain embellishments is *de rigueur*."

"What does that have to do with the occult?"

"There is no direct connection that I am aware of, but it may be that the two elements are juxtaposed in time. I say that because the Mathers Society seems to model itself on the Hermetic Order of the Golden Dawn, but that's just a guess."

"The Hermetic what?"

"A famous occult group active in Great Britain during the late nineteenth and early twentieth centuries. It had a number of distinguished members, including William Butler Yeats, Bram Stoker and Aleister Crowley. So you see, there's a chronological overlap between the Golden Dawn and Steampunk."

"How do you know all this?"

"Because I was a strange but exceptionally intelligent child in the deep South. Now then, what are you going to wear?"

"I have no idea. I don't own anything that looks even vaguely like what you're wearing."

"What about that Dracula outfit you wore for Halloween?"

"All right. I suppose we can try that." Cummings returned a few minutes later decked out as a vampire. "What do you think?"

"I would not bother with the fangs," Luther suggested. "People might think you are not taking them seriously."

Three

Chicago is a francized American Indian word meaning "stinky onion," a reference to a malodorous native plant. Stench is an echt metaphor for the history of Chicago.

Chicago might as well be a biblical city of plagues. Built on a bog, the early city was prone to insect-borne diseases, and the spring mud made parts of the town impassable. Later, there were sewer and water problems, followed by fire, riots, slaughterhouses, and graft. Fortunately, there was also vibrant commerce and robust architecture, or everyone would have fled the place.

Of Chicago's various maladies, graft is the most enduring. In some years one needs two hands worth of fingers to count the major political scandals and several bodies of fingers and toes to account for the minor ones. An even deeper problem is patronage. This frequently results in pervasive incompetence, exacerbated by Midwestern practicality. Once someone has an ill-gotten job, they tend to stay until death. Often they stay much longer.

Still, Chicago has its compensations: a veneer of progressive politics, affability, affordability, a lack of pretension, and stellar arts and culture. In the few years since moving to Chicago to be with Odin, Cummings had decided the city suited him as well as most places and better than many might have.

Even though it was Sunday morning, Cummings and Luther encountered traffic. Livestock were once packed in pens near the city's slaughterhouses, waiting to die; today, humans have a similar experience on Chicago roads.

As they sat in traffic Cummings proposed a number of routes but could not decide which made the most sense. He set his timer for five minutes and considered the various merits of each. When the buzzer sounded, and he could not decide on one, he let Luther make the call.

Eventually they arrived at their destination in the Bucktown neighborhood. Luther parked, and they walked a few blocks to an English-style pub called the Red and White.

The building, which was squeezed between a car wash and a funeral parlor, was an old Chicago commercial building; it was small, about a century old, made of red brick, and now painted a currently stylish shade of brownish beige. The sidewalk outside the main door was decorated with an elaborate medallion of red and white roses. These referred to the War of the Roses, the fifteenth-century English dynastic feud between rival factions in the House of Plantagenet: Lancaster (symbolized by a heraldic red rose) and York (represented by a white rose).

The décor inside was more William Morris than Henry Tudor. The walls were covered in ornate floral wallpapers, and the furnishings were heavy, wooden and overstuffed. On one side of the room, a great oak bar and surrounding lounge area circled an extravagantly tiled fireplace. The dining area, a phalanx of oak tables and chairs, was on the other side.

"We are going to a private room upstairs," Luther informed Cummings, indicating wide, dark oak stairs at the far end of the space.

Cummings looked up from the bottom of the stairs. The walls were a dark purple, and the interior lighting was dim.

Arriving at the top, they emerged into another seating area surrounding another Arts and Crafts fireplace. To the right, down a dimly lit purple passage, there was a door flanked by picture windows that revealed a large outdoor roof deck. To the left was a long bar. There were French doors at the far end, presently open, leading into the private dining room. From it, they heard a cacophony of indistinct conversations that grew louder as they approached.

The private dining room was large, carpeted in blood red wool, swirled with complex paisley patterns in tourmaline, canary, chocolate and black. The windows were covered in the heaviest red velvet, blocking even the possibility of light, while the walls were slathered with red damask wallpaper reminiscent of an 1890s New Orleans cathouse. Freestanding bronze censers at each corner of the room emitted languid clouds of Dragon's Blood incense.

The center of the room was dominated by a massive walnut dining table with marquetry inlays of cavorting peasants, flanked by thirty-two chairs, fifteen on each side and one on each end. A walnut podium stood near one end of the table.

Most of the chairs were filled with ladies and gentlemen in Neo-Edwardian garb, their outfits not precisely historical due to the presence of odd accessories: aviator goggles; metal face masks; World War I gas masks; multi-lensed monocles; walking sticks topped with skulls, black ravens, pentacles, runes, and other oddities; grotesquely overplumed women's millinery, and men's black top hats embedded with gears and washers. Cummings assumed these were the Steampunk embellishments to which Luther had referred.

A bit overwhelmed by the Alice-in-Wonderland-meets-opium-den environment, Luther and Cummings moved cautiously toward two empty chairs at the podium end of the table.

Cummings noticed an odd mixture of scents. At first he thought it was just the billowing incense. After sniffing a few times, he suspected there was also something else, but he wasn't sure what.

"Oh, look, there's Anunciación," Luther said, pointing to an imposing woman on the other side of the table. She smiled and came toward them.

Anunciación was a charismatic, *zaftig* older woman who made one think of Rodin's statue of Balzac. She had henna-dyed hair and dark brown eyes accentuated with liberal applications of kohl. Her long and menacingly sharp fingernails were lacquered Chinese red. A friendly but cryptic smile suggested she had reached the age of wisdom but wasn't sharing what she knew. She wore a long, white lace gown and white shoes, and her hair was swept up and embedded with flowers. Diaphanous fairy wings extended from her shoulders.

"Isn't this the most marvelous frock?" she said in a hybrid accent, two-thirds Midwestern American and one-third tony English. She slowly turned and modeled the outfit for Luther. "It's Titania's costume from an 1898 London production of *A Midsummer Night's Dream*. I bought it at auction."

"You are just dazzling!" Luther said appreciatively. Anunciación shrugged with artfully feigned modesty. "May I introduce my dear friend, Cummings Flynn Wanamaker? Cummings, this is Anunciación Hollingberry."

"It's nice to meet you. You have an interesting name," Cummings commented.

"People often say that, but there is a sensible explanation, don't you know," Anunciación replied. "I am the result of a coupling in a cave during the Spanish Civil War of an English prima ballerina and a Republican soldier."

"Really? How did an English ballerina find herself in a cave?"

"Stalactites," Anunciación continued. "Mama was also an amateur speleologist. She acquired this interest as a child whilst assisting grandfather in the collection of bat dung. Quite the best thing for the garden, don't you know. And what is your provenance, Cummings?"

"Eastern European and Jewish," Cummings responded. "I am named for E. E. Cummings and Errol Flynn. My father liked word play, and my mother liked sword play."

"Isn't that charming? Have you and Luther been introduced to the assembled?"

"Not yet," Cummings replied.

Anunciación clapped her hands several times. The conversation stopped, and all eyes shifted in her direction.

"We are among virgins, don't you know! These gentlemen are new to us at Mathers," Anunciación announced. "This is Luther Bannockburn and his friend, Cummings Flynn Wanamaker. Perhaps we could introduce ourselves. Winky, why don't you start?" She indicated a muscular man to Luther's immediate left. His ginger hair and sallow complexion seemed at odds with his flowing black poet shirt, jodhpurs and knee-high black leather boots.

"I'm Winky Carmello. This is my husband, Crandall Hobb," Winky said, referring to a middle-aged man sitting next to him, perhaps of Japanese descent, with long graying dreadlocks and a gray goatee. He was dressed in a black morning suit and top hat, giving him the appearance of an Edwardian undertaker. A pair of goggles hung around his neck, and he wore a pair of rubber "mad scientist" gloves.

"That's Lolita Gobble next to Crandall," Anunciación said, "and her husband, Rothwell Falconer, next to her."

Lolita, who had the angularity and height of a Giacometti sculpture, wore a pageboy haircut dyed a rather tawdry shade of pink. She wore a draped gown, more Ancient Greece than

Edwardian England, that fastened over her left shoulder, leaving her right arm and shoulder exposed. A flock of birds tattooed in a delicate shade of midnight blue flew across this shoulder.

Rothwell, who was also tall, was lightly muscled and intensely blonde; indeed, his hair was almost white. His skin was a pale alabaster, giving him the appearance of someone who rarely ventured outdoors. Ironically, he was dressed for exploring in the tropics in a khaki military suit with a jacket, jodhpurs, knee-high boots, and a white shirt and dark brown tie. His head was covered by a pith helmet and his eyes were framed with goggles.

On the other side of Rothwell, a woman sat in a Victorian wedding gown, complete with lace veil and train. "That's our speaker today, Surendra Hickok," Anunciación explained. "Dear, who is your companion?"

"I'm Rutley Paik. Hello, everybody," he said. Like many of the gentlemen, he wore an Edwardian morning coat. However, his was scarlet red and worn over a pair of jeans and red athletic shoes. Cummings noticed he was tall, red-haired, clean-shaven, a bit pudgy and quite handsome. Something about his physiognomy suggested a man far too practical to be dallying with these eccentrics.

"Rutley is ..." Surendra began, then hesitated for a moment before starting the sentence over. "Rutley is an old friend."

"We are also graced by the presence of Queen Victoria, otherwise known as Tom Daniels," Anunciación continued, referring to an excessively thin man in drag at the end of the table. He had bloodshot eyes the color of cooling lava and was dressed in an ornate black gown. Atop his head, a brown wig was pulled into a tight bun and covered with a lace cap. Like Victoria herself, his features were irregular and uninviting. His nose was overly prominent, and his lips seemed to express indiscriminate contempt. He was presently coughing into a white lace handkerchief.

Cummings noticed that three chairs at the table were empty. Anunciación looked in their direction and exclaimed, "Otto and Sebastian are late again!"

"Do you mean Otto Verissimo and his husband?"

"Who else? They are incapable of arriving on time, don't you know," Anunciación said with distaste. "I think we should move on to the victuals." She picked up a handbell from the podium and rang it three times. Waitresses appeared from the twenty-first century with computer-printed menus.

"Why does everyone have such exotic names?" Cummings whispered to Luther.

"I think it is part of the Steampunk aesthetic," Luther whispered back. "Fantasy clothes, fantasy personas."

"I see. And who is Otto Verissimo?" Cummings responded.

"The writer," Luther answered.

"Do you know him?"

"Not personally, but I am a devoted fan."

"What does he write?" Cummings asked.

"He is the author of our finest queer romance novels," Luther said. "You must have heard of him. They call him the gay Barbara Cartland."

"Who is Barbara Cartland?" Cummings asked.

"Do you mean to tell me you have never heard of Barbara Cartland?"

"No. Should I have?"

Luther glanced at Cummings in a manner that conveyed both pity and horror, and then he shifted his attention to selecting a sandwich.

Some minutes later, three men entered the room.

The first man was dressed as a Prussian military officer, in a smart blue coat heavy with metals, a spiked helmet, tight black trousers, and knee-high boots. One of his arms was covered in brass armor adorned with cogs, wheels, and grommets. This man was perhaps thirty-five and not a beauty: he had a broad forehead, bushy brows, eyes that were too small, a nose that was too large, and pitted, oleaginous skin. He moved in a languid but graceful manner.

The second man, who was perhaps forty-five, tall, hirsute, chubby, and had a beard, was dressed as an Edwardian minister. He wore a severe black suit and a clerical collar. A Christian cross, which descended from a gold chain around his neck, was adorned with spokes and gears. His round, slightly asymmetrical face wasn't exactly handsome, but he exuded the dispassionate authority that suggests a forceful leader. This gave him a certain sexiness.

The third man, who was focused on photographing the other two, looked like a hobbit that had emigrated to Israel. He was rotund, short and in early middle age. His pate was bald and covered by a yarmulke. From just above his ears, carrot-colored hair, frizzled as if it had been electrified, descended a foot or more. A long beard, robust and streaked with gray, cascaded from his chin. He wore a white button shirt, a tartan kilt, and highland boots.

"Otto!" Anunciación said to the first man. "We've gone ahead and ordered."

"I am so sorry to be tardy," Otto said in a wispy, nasal voice. "There was a bit of a crisis. My cologne atomizer clogged."

"That is Otto Verissimo," Luther, awestruck, whispered to Cummings.

"Who are the other men?" Cummings whispered back.

"The second man must be his husband, Sebastian Grinnell. He owns a few bars in Boys Town. I don't know who the red-haired one is," Luther said.

Anunciación had everyone introduce themselves again, and then lunch was served. An hour later it was cleared away. Anunciación rang her bell again and called the meeting to order.

"As the President of the Samuel Liddell MacGregor Mathers Society, I am very pleased to welcome you to our 245th monthly meeting. As many of you know, Mathers was an English occultist of the Edwardian era. He was a radical vegetarian, an early translator of neglected occult texts, and using his mediumistic talents, a passionate player of chess with the Gods. Unfortunately, he did not leave a record of his wins and losses.

"The Mathers Society meets once a month to advance the knowledge of the arcane. We dance with the unusual and delight in the obscure, don't you know. When it appeared about ten years ago, we embraced Steampunk as a modern aesthetic reinterpretation of the English occult consciousness we bring from the past. Thus, we have fused these elements in a historical yet modern whole."

Cummings coughed. He wished someone would put out the incense.

"We are privileged today," Anunciación continued, "for another presentation in our mini-series on famous women of the occult. As you all know, Surendra Hickok is a historian of the occult and the author of a biography of Wilhelm Reich. Today, she will speak on her latest project, a biography of Ida Craddock. Surendra?"

Surendra strode to the podium and planted herself confidently before the microphone. She lifted her bridal veil.

"Good afternoon, everybody. Thank you for coming. For those of you who don't know me, I'm Surendra Hickok. My passion is writing biographies. I've published two. The first, co-authored with my sister, was on the early twentieth-century astrologer, Evangeline Adams. Last year I completed a study of Wilhelm Reich, the renegade disciple of Freud and inventor of the orgone. I am now working on a biography of Ida Craddock. How many of you recognize that name?"

A number of hands went up. This impressed Cummings, as he had no idea who Ida Craddock was. He'd never heard of Evangeline Adams either. Wilhelm Reich's name sounded somewhat familiar, though he was sure he couldn't have accurately identified him.

"Ida Craddock was a nineteenth-century mystic and sexual explorer, born in Philadelphia in 1857. She would have been the first female admitted to the University of Pennsylvania, had the Trustees not blocked her admission. At around the age of thirty, she became active in the Theosophical Society. As most of you know, the Theosophical Society was founded in New York City in 1875 to investigate the nature of the universe and humanity's place in it. In their sheltering arms Ida studied the sexual wisdom paths of various traditions, such as tantra."

"What's a sexual wisdom path?" Cummings whispered to Luther.

"I do not have any idea, but it does not sound Baptist," Luther whispered back.

"Ultimately she said she had married and had an active sexual life with an angel named Soph," Hickok continued. "Of course it is difficult for most of us to imagine this, but she seemed to be insistent about it. I'm wearing this wedding dress today to acknowledge Ida's truth, even though I can't claim to truly understand it myself. I'm also wearing the Craddock brooch." She indicated a pendant on a chain about her neck. "It is said to have healing properties.

"Eventually Ida opened an office in Chicago to offer sexual counseling to married couples, a truly radical undertaking in Ida's time. She wrote widely on the subject of marital sexuality, achieving sufficient notoriety by 1899 to run into legal persecution, notably from Anthony Comstock. He, of course, was the founder of the New York Society for the Suppression of Vice, a ruthless public moralist.

"She was convicted and sentenced to federal prison in 1902 and committed suicide the night before she was to begin her sentence.

"This overview cannot capture the full range of Ms. Craddock's contributions to ..."

Surendra Hickok stopped and coughed. Cummings noticed that the smoke in the room seemed suddenly to have increased in density.

"They really might cut back on the incense," Cummings thought.

"Craddock's contributions to the ..." Surendra stammered, trying to continue. She couldn't. She abruptly screamed. Her wedding dress had erupted in fire.

Cummings scanned the room. The cause of the smoke wasn't the incense. The velvet drapes were smoking heavily and starting to flame.

Rutley Paik pulled off his morning coat and leapt at Surendra, attempting to smother the flames.

Tom tossed drinks and water at Surendra and then at the drapes.

Crandall and Sebastian called for help on their cell phones.

Winky shrieked and stood frozen, while Tom and Otto moved at great speed for no particular reason in no particular direction, bumping into the furniture and other Mathers members.

Anunciación ran toward the French doors in a panic and then hesitated, blocking the exit until Lolita pushed her out of the way.

The Scottish-Jewish hobbit *davenned*.

Meanwhile, the flames had begun to spread throughout the room.

Half an hour later, from the safety of the sidewalk across the street, the group of stunned Neo-Edwardians watched the Chicago Fire Department try to save what was left of the Red and White. Many Mathers members had minor injuries, mostly smoke inhalation, and were being treated by paramedics. No one was deemed sufficiently afflicted to require a trip to the hospital. The burnt remains of the one casualty, Surendra Hickok, were loaded into an ambulance.

Police circulated; they asked individuals what they had observed and took names and contact information. Finally they suggested that everyone go home.

"I think we may as well leave now," Luther stammered to Cummings, his voice tremulous. "Yes, I think we may as well," he repeated. Cummings nodded, and they turned in the direction of Cummings's car.

Cummings felt a tug on his sleeve.

"I don't think we've met—not exactly." It was Otto Verissimo.

"I know who you are," Cummings replied.

"Do you? And I know who you are. I recognize your name from the article in the *Tribune*. You're that accomplished amateur detective."

"Yes," Cummings said.

"I need to consult you," Otto said, lowering his voice to a whisper, "as soon as possible. Please!" Otto thrust an elegantly printed business card into Cummings's hand and disappeared into the crowd.

Four

The next morning Cummings was in the kitchen, perusing tea canisters as the summer sun rose to smother Chicago with another day of heat and humidity. Cummings and Odin were quite the tea aficionados and always kept twelve small numbered canisters of different varieties in their kitchen.

Cummings studied the canisters, trying to decide which tea he wanted. Unsure, he retrieved a pair of dice he kept in a drawer and threw them. The winner was canister four, Irish Breakfast Tea.

He had emailed Otto and set up an appointment for that afternoon. As his tea steeped he searched the Internet to see what he could find about Otto Verissimo.

It seemed that Otto was a very successful author, although an article in *Publishers Weekly* suggested that his books, like those of any number of other genre writers, were experiencing flat sales in the economic downturn. Otto's husband, Sebastian Grinnell, whom he had married in Provincetown the year before, owned three thriving bars on Halsted Street in Lakeview, Chicago's historic gay neighborhood, known colloquially as Boys Town. Even in the Great Recession of the early twenty-first century, this was not a couple struggling to pay the bills.

Next Cummings turned to the first page of *The Curse of Manley Abbey,* a novel by Otto Verissimo that Cummings had borrowed from Luther the previous day:

Master Hamilton is remarkable for his good humor. Were he even ugly, one could not help being pleased with him. He is possessed of a sterling sweetness of temper, and his person is genteel, his complexion fair, and his physique delightful. He is indeed a very fit young man to be taken off the town, as he would be an agreeable companion. The God of Love seems to have intended a better fate for his charms than prostitution."

Such was Master Hamilton's listing in *Covent Garden Sodomites, or a man of pleasure's calendar,* for the year 1775, the London directory of gentlemen of the evening. It was this that first brought Sir Reginald Manley to seek out Master Hamilton's acquaintance. Although Sir Manley was an esteemed and fine person, with a generous turn of mind, he was not above temptation from either the fair or the virile sex.

Even at the first, there was considerable felicity between them. This natural affection, along with Sir Reginald's endowment of Christian virtue, led him to manly restraint when first he met the lad. Rather than taking his pleasure with Master Hamilton, Sir Reginald called for a pot of tea and inquired as to the young man's upbringing and education.

"I possess a knowledge of Latin and Greek, sir," Hamilton replied, "and of mathematics, the sciences, music, and drawing. As to my parentage, sir, this is unknown. I was taken in as a foundling and raised in a heathen land by a missionary and his wife. I would be with them still but that they were trampled by a distraught water buffalo whilst engaged in a particularly fervent baptism. After my benefactors were thus martyred, I used what little legacy they left me to return to England."

"A great tragedy," Sir Reginald said sympathetically. "Have you never sought a position as tutor to some well-

bred family? Surely, such employment would raise you up from your present condition."

"Alas, sir, my penury was so extraordinary that I had no recourse but to embark upon my present path. And now, having trod this path of despond, what good family may consider me suitable?"

"You must not despair for our Lord is just and gracious, and does not assent to the black passions of humanity. The mercy he has placed in each human bosom will, through pity, be awakened in all but the most cruel," Sir Reginald replied, gracefully extending his patrician hand in the direction of the teapot. *"I am a widower with two daughters, Pamela and Clarissa. Our home is Manley Abbey,"* he continued, delicately emptying the amber liquid into porcelain cups emblazoned with the seven virtues, of which Sir Reginald most prized humility. *"They are in need of instruction and guidance just now after the most unfortunate death of their late governess, a Miss Bentham, who disappeared suddenly from a cottage on the estate."*

"Disappeared, sir?"

"Indeed. We fear she belonged to an Irish secret society. More than that, I cannot say."

"Most unfortunate," Master Hamilton replied, not presuming to enquire further.

"I believe you to be a young man of rare quality and virtue," Sir Reginald opined, *"who wouldst well please my daughters and myself. What say you to coming into my service?"* Sir Reginald proposed.

"Oh sir, I should be delighted," the young man replied quietly but enthusiastically, his youthful, well-formed physique shivering slightly with gratitude.

Even though his aesthetic instincts were rudimentary, since Cummings hadn't received the arts and culture genes seemingly so prevalent in the gay male population, he knew that this particular literary work was not destined for immortality.

Cummings abandoned Otto's prose and moved on to the morning's *Chicago Tribune.* On page three he discovered a brief report of Surendra's death. This led him to reach for his cell phone.

"Rockland, it's Cummings. I'm calling to check on Luther."

"Why? Has he done something naughty?"

"He seemed quite shaken up by the Mathers fire."

"I know. I'm being humorous. Yes, yes, he's a sensitive boy. I am pleased to report that he's fine and is on his way to work. Now, what's all this nonsense I read in the *Tribune* about spontaneous combustion?"

"Don't you think it's possible?"

"Of course not."

"I think there was an accelerant," Cummings concurred. "I believe I smelled something suspicious."

"Can you be more precise?" Rockland asked.

"It's difficult to say because the air was full of incense and then smoke from the fire. However, I think I detected an oily undercurrent. I'm wondering if it was linseed oil. Rags soaked in it can self-combust. Of course, they'd have to be saturated and left to sit for a while, perhaps an hour or more, before they ignited. Linseed oil is sometimes used to finish wood. When I lived in Maine, someone left linseed-saturated rags on the floor in a shop in the village I lived in, and the place burned down."

"Of course, there are many flammable substances," Rockland suggested.

"Yes, there are," Cummings agreed, "but let's suppose someone wanted to kill Surendra. Everyone wears antique or reproduction clothes to the Mathers Society, admittedly augmented with Steampunk motifs. For women that means long dresses. If the murderer left linseed-saturated rags in the base of the lectern at which Surendra was standing, he might reasonably suppose her dress would catch on fire."

"Wouldn't she notice the smell?"

"Not necessarily. She might not have recognized the odor as a dangerous substance. Or perhaps her dress had been stored in moth balls, a very strong scent."

"I suppose it's possible," Rockland said, "but it seems a particularly gruesome way to kill someone and, I might add, a rather questionable strategy. The flames could easily have been put out."

"All of that is true," Cummings agreed. "I'm just speculating, but I also have to say this: people like us, who tend to be rational, often assume that everyone else tends to be rational, too. We sometimes eliminate strategies as absurd because they're illogical, but others may not view it that way. Does that seem overly cynical?"

"What you say reminds me of the Nero responses."

"What's that?"

"A joke I heard from a philosophy professor when I was an undergrad. I can't tell jokes properly, but the idea is that in a crisis—Rome burning, in this instance—four possible responses emerge. The first is to fiddle, which is the accommodation of the idealist. The second is to let the city burn; that's what the fatalist does. The pragmatist, the third option, puts out the fire. And the fourth reaction, that of the nihilist, is to the kill the fiddler. You will note that any of these four might argue that he is behaving rationally, but only one reaction seems objectively rational, that of the pragmatist, because it's the only action that minimizes harm. People will always do what makes sense to *them*, but that is not always what makes sense."

"True enough, though as jokes go, that one isn't particularly amusing."

"Perhaps it is if you're a philosophy professor."

"Please tell Luther I phoned."

"I shall," Rockland promised. "Don't forget to phone me if you run into something less incendiary and more biochemical. Poison—that's what gets my blood flowing!"

The next morning Cummings had an interview with a prospective consulting client. He put on his best dark suit and reflected on how nervous he was. Suspect interviews were one thing; selling himself was something else.

He drove to a large, modern apartment building in Lincoln Park, Chicago's toniest neighborhood, parked his car and announced himself to the doorman. Cummings was directed to the elevator and soon found himself seated across from Mrs. Bernice Randall in her spacious home office.

She appeared to have the tight skin and loose thinking Cummings had come to associate with old money, along with the requisite elegant coif, tasteful tailoring, and slightly ostentatious jewelry. The apartment was on a high floor, and the room had magnificent views of Lake Michigan. There was a modern chrome and glass desk; bookcases dotted with family photographs and knick-knacks and even a few actual books; and on a nearby wall, an oil portrait of a woman in a beaded dress from the 1920s.

"Is that your grandmother?" Cummings suggested. "She must have been an inspiration to you."

"Yes. How did you know that?"

"She's wearing the same bracelet as you are. My assumption is that such an heirloom would likely pass across generations from mother to daughter. I surmise you are either your mother's only daughter or her eldest daughter. Since you've given the portrait a place of prominence in your office, I imagine you admired your grandmother."

"Aren't you clever?" Mrs. Randall said, pleased. "I can see why you're highly recommended."

"Thank you," he said. He wasn't actually sure how she'd gotten his name, probably someone who knew someone who knew someone. He'd been working in philanthropy for a long time.

"You know, we're a small family foundation. We're not terribly strategic. We fund health care, education, the environment, the arts—the usual areas."

"Yes. I've done a little research on you," Cummings said.

"We're looking for a consultant to help us evaluate the impact of our funding."

"I see, and what kind of impact are you seeking to evaluate?"

"Well, we've given out twelve million dollars in the last five years, and we have no idea if it's done any good."

"I meant, what do you mean by 'impact,' and what do you mean by 'good'? Do you mean you'd like to know if your money helped immediate circumstances or if it actually helped to solve difficult problems?"

"Those are excellent questions. That's what we want to find out."

"I see. Well, it's fairly easy to assess if giving away money has an impact on current conditions, but it's almost impossible to say if you're helping to conquer larger problems. The problem is trying to connect the dots with straight lines, avoiding what they call confounding variables in statistics."

"I assume you're not saying that philanthropy is a waste of time?" Mrs. Randall said, a slight unease in her voice.

"No, no. Giving money to, say, disaster relief will certainly help to ease immediate suffering, but can you really know if your donation to, say, hurricane forecasting research is critical to a breakthrough that emerges? In most cases you can't."

"Then what is one to do?"

"That's a good question. If I may use a metaphor, I'd say it's like your failed marriage."

"How did you know about that?" she said, startled.

"The slight puffiness around the ring finger on your left hand. There was a ring there that you've taken off."

"What does hurricane forecasting have to do with my divorce?"

"Perhaps I'm not being clear. A better analogy might be your strained relationship with your son."

"What?"

"I read your biography. You have a daughter and a son. I see many pictures of her but none of him. My point is, philanthropy is like a difficult relationship; you keep making the effort because it's important and hope that eventually things will change."

"I'm sorry," she said, standing suddenly. "I don't think this will be a good fit."

"Oh," Cummings said, surprised by her abruptness. "Well, thank you for your time."

After this debacle Cummings stopped for a quick sandwich. He reflected painfully on what had just happened with Mrs. Randall. He set the timer on his wristwatch and considered why he always seemed to say the wrong thing in such circumstances. By the time the buzzer went off, he had concluded that perhaps relaxation techniques might improve his interpersonal skills. He determined to get a book on client interviewing and see if he could improve.

He looked at his watch and realized that he was due soon at Otto's.

Otto Verissimo lived in the Prairie Avenue Historic District, the section of the near South Side that housed Chicago's wealthiest families in the late nineteenth century. Today the area is part of Chicago's South Loop. Where there were once mansions, there are now condominia, though a few of the old mansions remain. Otto lived in one of these, a house commonly known by architectural preservationists, of which there are many in Chicago, as the Ogalala Castle. A gothic curiosity, it was built in 1894 by Harrison Glendenning, a patent medicine magnate, and his wife.

Mrs. Glendenning designed the home herself after the famous Chicago architect Louis Sullivan refused to work with her. Her taste was more exuberant than informed; it was based on one grand tour of the Continent and a small collection of stereopticon slides. Local architectural historians often write that the house is a poor example of late Gothic Revival, but what they really mean is that it's a monstrosity. Its facade is a cacophony of arches, flying buttresses, stained glass, martyrs and gargoyles. The interior is primarily ebony, so pervasive and dark that masses of electric light have little noticeable effect.

In 1920 all but one of the Glendennings perished in a boating accident on Lake Michigan. Only Ogalala Glendenning, ten years old at the time, survived by clinging to her mother's lifeless but buoyant body. Ogalala was so traumatized that she never spoke a word again. She died in

1985 without heirs, and the house deteriorated until Otto and Sebastian purchased it in 1990.

It is difficult to say what attracted Otto and Sebastian to the Castle. One likes to imagine that Mrs. Glendenning's passionate lack of discernment struck them as the perfect complement for Otto's artless but heartfelt prose. However, this assumes a self-awareness that artists, particularly bad ones, rarely possess. More likely, Otto saw the grand where others saw the garish, and to keep the peace, Sebastian went along with Otto's vision.

During a three-year rehabilitation, Otto and Sebastian updated the wiring and plumbing, put in a functional kitchen and generally restored the house to its original state of pseudo-historical Gothic hysteria. It had been their home since.

This was, of course, Cummings's first visit to the Castle. As all new visitors are, he was a bit overwhelmed by its strange combination of ostentation and gloom. He approached the front door and depressed the buzzer. This resulted in an anemic electronic chirp.

The hobbit-like creature, last seen photographing Otto at the Mathers Society, opened the door. Cummings noticed he was wearing the same kilt and yarmulke. The man raised his frizzled ginger eyebrows in greeting and spoke in a thick Scottish accent.

"Guid morning! Hou's aw wi ye? Are ye famischt?"

Cummings did not have any idea what had just been said to him. Fortunately, the man raised his arm in a gesture of welcome, and Cummings understood he was being invited to enter.

Cummings found himself in a large entry hall with marble floors in a morose gray, ceilings a slightly lighter shade of the same color and darkly stained paneling on the walls. A collection of mounted stuffed heads—lion, elk, tiger and cheetah—hung high up on the paneling. These creatures seemed to gaze down intensely, as if to remind visitors that they might end up as lunch. A massive chandelier illuminated the space, but only enough to allow for a cautious passage further into the house. Otto Verissimo stood nearby wearing a vivid lilac smoking jacket.

"This is quite a house," Cummings said.

"Do you like it? I think of it as something between a castle and a cathedral, sort of a relic of the true schloss," he said in a vaporous voice, smirking at his obscure pun.

"Did you shoot those yourself?" Cummings asked playfully.

"Sebastian's grandfather did. He was a shooting buddy of Ernest Hemingway."

"Was he?"

"I'm afraid so. Sebastian insisted we put them up. Mandrake, tea in the Parlor of the Orchids, I think."

Mandrake nodded and scurried off.

"That gentleman—I assume he's your assistant?"

"Mandrake is my personal assistant. I find him quite delightful, but perhaps I should warn you that some people find him a bit odd," Otto confided to Cummings as he led him down the hall. "It seems Mandrake was born in Scotland, but he was taken as a small child to Minnesota, where he was raised by religious Jews. The rest is lost in the mists of his personal history."

A miniature poodle appeared in the hallway, groomed, as all self-respecting poodles are, to resemble the topiary at Versailles. It approached Otto with a certain haughtiness and stood by his side. Otto's husband, whom Cummings remembered from the Mathers meeting, followed a few moments later.

"This is Barbara Cartland," Otto announced, indicating the poodle. Barbara approached Cummings and imperiously sniffed his crotch. "And this is my husband, Sebastian Grinnell."

"I remember seeing you at the Mathers event. It's tragic what happened," Sebastian said, extending his hand to Cummings with a well-practiced professional smile. They shook. "You must excuse me. I'm late for a meeting." He leaned over and kissed Otto. "I'll be home early," he said and walked toward the front door.

What kind of man introduces his dog before his husband? Cummings wondered, while he said, "I think I've heard the name Barbara Cartland. She was some kind of writer, wasn't she?"

"She was the most successful writer of romance novels the world has ever known! She passed over in 2000. She's very much missed."

Otto stopped in front of a pair of heavy oak doors and flung them open. Inside was another dark room, primarily illuminated by colored light filtering in through various stained glass windows. The room was painted red and featured a massive stone fireplace carved with scenes of assorted Christian martyrs meeting horrible deaths. The room was populated with heavy Jacobean furniture, on every flat surface of which were massed various species of black orchids.

"Please sit down," Otto said as Mandrake wheeled a silver teacart into the room and left. His camera hung from a cord around his neck.

"Tea?"

"Thank you."

"Would you like some rugelach? Mandrake bakes it fresh every morning."

As he sipped his tea and munched on prune rugelach, Mandrake took several photos.

"You don't mind a few pictures, do you? We like to document everything I do. It's so useful for publicity."

Cummings observed a carved bookcase nearby. All the books displayed appeared to be Otto's: hard covers, paperbacks, translations, special deluxe editions and box sets.

"You must be quite prolific," Cummings said.

"Barbara Cartland published seven hundred twenty-three books in her lifetime, and she left another one hundred fifty manuscripts behind. I've only managed eighty-four novels to date. Years ago I wrote rather conventional heterosexual romances, but in the last few years I've been blessed to pioneer the gay historical romance sub-genre."

"I understand you're quite popular. My friend Luther is very fond of your books."

"Is he?" Otto said with a hint of a smile. He stood and yanked twice on a velvet bell pull near the door. A few moments later, Mandrake appeared, wheeling another silver cart. This one contained neatly piled stacks of hard cover books.

"Perhaps he'd like an autographed copy of my latest, *The Hirsute Cavalier*. Luther, was it?"

Otto picked up a fountain pen from the cart. He elegantly inscribed a volume and handed it to Cummings.

"Thank you," Cummings said. "I'm sure he will be delighted."

"You're quite welcome." Otto nodded his head in Mandrake's direction, who understood this to be his cue to exit the room.

"I'm sure you're wondering why I asked to meet with you," Otto said as soon as Mandrake was gone. "I want you to find the brooch."

"Do you mean the pendant the victim was wearing?"

"Yes. It's called the Craddock Brooch. Somehow it disappeared in the fire."

"Why are you interested in it?"

"It's a cherished pagan reliquary, a piece of Ida Craddock's leg bone. Pagan reliquaries are quite rare, you know. It's mostly the Catholics who go in for that sort of thing."

"How do you know it's disappeared?"

Otto seemed startled by the question. "It wasn't on the body, nor was it in the room. People looked for it."

"How is it possible anyone could have searched? The fire spread very quickly. No one would have had time."

"Someone snuck in and searched that night," Otto explained with slight hesitation. This led Cummings to wonder if he was making the plot line up on the spot.

"Why would someone take that risk?"

"As I said, the brooch is rare. I assure you that it's gone. Can you help us?"

"Perhaps. May I ask you some questions? How well did you know the victim?"

Before Otto could respond Mandrake entered the room and said something to Otto that was incomprehensible, at least to Cummings.

"Oh, my! Apparently I am terribly late for an appointment," Otto announced. "I'm counting on you, Cummings. You must help. You must. I'll be in contact."

"But I have a number of questions ..."

"We'll chat again soon!"

Mandrake showed Cummings to the door.

Cummings spent the afternoon following up leads for consulting jobs. None led to work. Subsequently he made a simple chicken and pasta dish, timed for Odin's arrival home from work.

"How was your day?" Cummings asked as Odin walked in.

"Another day in the salt mines," Odin said in a dejected tone.

"Did something happen?"

"I really don't want to talk just now," Odin said, pouring himself a Scotch.

Cummings let it go. They ate their dinner in silence.

Later the phone rang.

"Ernestine here. Is that you, Cummings?" a crisp female voice said. It was Ernestine Cutter, Cumming's only real friend in Horeb, Maine.

Ernestine was an elderly upper class New Englander, patrician and practical, stolid and well mannered. She was always polite but kept loaded guns in both of her Georgian sideboards.

She had been born a Biederman, one of Horeb's founding families, and was raised in the village. However, as a child she spent a lot of time with relatives in more remote parts of the state. This accounted for her vestigial Downeast accent, the disappearing patois of rural Maine. Except for these rural sojourns and attendance at Smith College, Ernestine had spent all of her seventy-odd years in Horeb. She had married Horeb's wealthiest citizen, Benjamin Cutter. Mister Cutter, as Ernestine referred to him when a reference to him couldn't be avoided, turned out to be a bore, a drunk and a pedophile, and not even in that order. Fortunately, she was now a widow.

As far as Cummings could tell, she had a great deal of money and the apparent forgiveness of her neighbors for her husband's heinous acts. The price was a remorse that never left her.

She persevered as best she could. She read travel books, though she rarely travelled, as well as detective novels, though she and Cummings had solved the great crime of both of their lives: the murder of her son, Terry, her only child, with whom Cummings had had a long relationship.

"Ernestine, how nice to hear from you!"

"Perhaps not, dear. I am the bearer of wicked bad news. Chess Biederman is dead. They found his body in a boat."

"Really?" Cummings said, surprised.

"He disappeared in the fall and everyone thought the worst. Still, it cannot help but give you a grue when you rip the winter covering off of a dinghy and find a body, even these days when one is surprised only when nothing awful happens."

"Were you the one that found him?"

"No, dear. Elektra Philemon did. She's Deuteronomy Smelt's housekeeper. Did you ever meet him?"

"I heard about him. He's a recluse, isn't he? A writer of some sort."

"He used to write spy novels under the name of Nash Hammer. Elektra is his housekeeper. She and some local boys found the body. She didn't react well. I guess that's to be expected if your name is Elektra. One of the boys came to the house to get me right after they found Chess."

"Where was the boat?"

"On my land. I've allowed Deuty to keep his boat at my place for some years now. His books don't sell like they once did. It's no trouble to do it. It's just an old broken down lobster boat. It's moored to my dock during the summer, and we raise it onto the land during the winter."

"Why does he keep a boat if he's a recluse?"

"He likes the water. He just doesn't like to talk to people while he's floating on it. They say he goes out late at night with Elektra."

"I assume the death is suspicious?"

"Of course it's suspicious."

"Any word yet on the police investigation?"

"Officer Bernier's working on it." Bernier was a local sheriff of whom neither was overly fond. "He hasn't used the word murder, but a pterodactyl is not a tabby cat, even if they both have teeth. Word is there's going to be an autopsy. Anyway, you knew Chess, and I thought you'd want to be told."

It was true. Cummings did want to be told, but the reason was curiosity, not a deep connection to the deceased. Cummings barely knew Chess Biederman.

The first time they'd met, Chess had been sitting in what looked to Cummings to be a small armoire or perhaps a large pie safe, except that it didn't quite resemble either. It was oblong, about the size of a large refrigerator—perhaps six feet high, two feet wide and three-feet deep. It was constructed, or at least finished, in varnished wood. Its door was presently closed.

"What is that you're sitting in?" Cummings had asked.

"An orgone accumulator, sometimes called an orgone box," Chess responded. "I design and build them. Have you ever heard of Wilhelm Reich?

"No."

"He invented them," Chess explained. "He was a psychiatrist, one of Freud's disciples, and a renegade. He lived in Maine from the mid-1940s to the late '50s. Then the government threw him in prison, where he died. The theory is that by sitting in here for a half-hour a day, you accumulate life energy and vitality."

"And have you become more alive and vital?"

"Of course. I ejaculate with the force of a steam engine."

Their subsequent interactions had been sporadic but no less eccentric.

Drifting back to the present, Cummings exclaimed to Ernestine, "That's where I heard it!"

"Heard what?"

"Wilhelm Reich. He invented the orgone box."

"I wouldn't know about that, dear. I don't go in much for psychology. Life is hard enough without trying to understand why some people have to make it so much harder for everybody else," Ernestine said.

"When is the funeral?"

"The police still have the body, but the word is they will release it soon. I imagine next week. I'll let you know when I know."

"I'd appreciate that," Cummings said.

Five

Deuteronomy Smelt was retired now. He'd penned thirty-six thrillers under the name Nash Hammer. The first, *The Gun with the Platinum Woman*, had narrowly missed *The New York Times* Bestseller List in 1957. The last, *Tomorrow, Your Breasts*, was quickly remaindered in 2001. His current royalty checks, when they arrived, were hardly worth depositing. Still, between what little he'd saved from television and film sales, and money left to him by an aunt, he managed to get by.

Deuteronomy was more intelligent than talented and more strategic than adaptable. The 1950s and early 1960s had served him well, as they were full of memes he understood: gin, Communism, prosperity, seduction. By the 1970s he was struggling but keeping up, substituting marijuana for martinis, adding computers into his espionage toolkit and creating female characters with a diminished sense of moral order and extraordinarily large breasts.

By the 1990s, after the Cold War ended, the thrill had gone out of his thrillers. International terrorism, with its lack of nuance, held no interest for Deuteronomy. It lacked the vigor of Ernest Hemingway, the intrigue of Eric Ambler, the moral ambivalence of Graham Greene—even the testosterone of Mickey Spillane. Deuteronomy was a man who understood thinking twenty moves ahead in a struggle with Russian espionage. He did not understand the new world order in which ideological zealots wished only to blow up the game board.

Like Ernestine Cutter, Deuteronomy was born and raised in Horeb, the only child of an imperious English teacher who was widowed young. She insisted on unaccented American speech. Whatever tendencies Deuteronomy had toward a Downeast accent were drilled out of him.

He was now a widower and had a daughter who lived half a continent away. He rarely saw her. He didn't see much of Elektra either, who had been his housekeeper for many years and lived in the house. In fact he saw little of anyone. Since his wife Edwina's death about a decade earlier, he had gone out less and less. It was more a matter of disinterest than depression.

In the last few years he emerged only at night, usually in the summer, to take midnight boat rides. Otherwise, unless it was essential, he saw no one and spoke to no one. He relied on Elektra to manage all the practical elements of the household and his life. When communication was necessary, he often used postcards. There was no particular rationale for this idiosyncrasy. It was just what he did.

Deuteronomy had inherited the house, a large Victorian, from his mother. Her grandfather, a sea captain, had built the house in 1848. The sea captain had been wealthy, and the house reflected this. It had many large rooms on three floors plus a full attic, with a grand staircase in the middle ornately carved from Maine maple. Unfortunately, the sea captain's descendants were not wealthy, and they had struggled to provide the maintenance that such a house required. The home was still grand but had long since become shabby.

Deuteronomy spent much of his time in his bedroom, which was large and resembled a nineteenth-century English men's club. The walls were covered in late Victorian wallpaper in morose shades of blue and green, with navy blue, floor-to-ceiling velvet drapes. These were original to the house and in dire need of replacement. Deuteronomy wouldn't hear of redecorating, even during those periods when he could have afforded it. Somehow the deteriorating elegance suited him.

His bedroom was furnished with a massive oak bed, several leather lounge chairs, a wall of books and a large writing desk. On this sat a computer and a printer; both of these were distrusted but accepted as a part of the general cultural decline in which thoughtful men now found themselves. There was also an old hi-fi console, which Deuteronomy used to play classical records.

Most of his days passed uneventfully: He read, he thought, he wrote letters to his daughter or his few remaining friends, or he made notes for novels he would likely never write. At night he listened to music.

Deuteronomy—"Deuty" to his friends—had recently arisen. He was about to go to the dining room for his breakfast when Elektra, irate, burst into his bedroom without knocking. Fortunately, he was already dressed in black slacks, a grey herringbone jacket and a crisp white shirt with a striped bow tie.

"In boat dead body, is in plastic wrap like the leftover chicken!"

"What are you talking about?" Deuteronomy asked calmly. He was used to Elektra's theatrics and never allowed himself to succumb.

"Through whole winter maybe this body been in boat. Look to me it freeze and thaw, freeze and thaw, freeze and thaw. And the animals, they eat this body. Ugly!" Elektra continued with sweeping dramatic gestures evoking the probable rise and fall of the temperature. "But him I know. I see the big blue ring on finger. This is the ring it belong to Chess Biederman. I say this to the police."

"Do you mean that you've just discovered Chess Biederman's body on my boat?"

"Yes. Chess Biederman! <u>Nekra</u>! <u>Nekra</u>! <u>Nekra</u>! What is the word in the English?"

"Dead?"

"Yes! Him dead!"

"How was he killed? Suffocated? Stabbed? Shot? What?"

"I not knows this."

The door buzzer interrupted the conversation, an unusual occurrence in a household that had few visitors. That the front door had a buzzer, and was even used regularly, was somewhat unusual in rural New England. Because of the climate and perhaps for other reasons lost to history, the back door is the usual means of coming and going. This had to be an important call.

Elektra went to answer the door. After she did, Deuteronomy heard a male voice.

"The police here," Elektra announced anxiously as she returned to Deuteronomy's bedroom. "These police they come see you. In the parlor I put police."

"I don't feel like seeing anyone," he replied.

"Is the police!" Elektra exclaimed vehemently.

"Yes, I suppose you're right," Deuteronomy said, rising dutifully to face the inevitable. He straightened his bow tie and walked down the hall.

A uniformed policeman sat on Deuteronomy's sofa. The officer was perhaps forty, short, taut and muscular. He carried with him a canvas bag, which he'd set on the floor. From it he removed a half-finished doily and went to work on it with a crochet hook.

"What are you doing there?" Deuteronomy asked as he entered the room.

"Tatting. It reduces stress," the officer replied gruffly, setting down his handiwork and rising. "I'm Officer Bernier from the Sagadahoc County Sheriff's office. I transferred down here from Bangor a few years ago. I don't think we've met."

"No. I don't go out much. I'm Deuteronomy Smelt, but presumably you know that. You may refer to me as Mister Smelt or Deuty, as you wish."

They shook hands. Officer Bernier sat and resumed tatting.

"I understand Chess Biederman's body has been found on my boat," Deuteronomy said.

"That's correct."

"Are you absolutely sure that's who it is? I ask only because my housekeeper informs me that the body was both desiccated and disturbed by animals."

"He was wearing a ring known to belong to Chess Biederman, and we have dental records. Also, as you likely know, Chess disappeared in the fall, and no one has seen him since."

"I assume you're here because you think Chess was murdered?"

"We're awaiting autopsy results."

"But what's your gut instinct?"

"My gut instinct is to wait for the autopsy results."

"Of course, of course. Still, it could be the result of natural causes, couldn't it? I recall that Chess was prone to a number of allergies as a child, though I can't remember any longer to what he was allergic. I do remember my late wife commiserating with Chess's mother about his health, the way women do."

"If Chess died from an allergic reaction, why was his body hidden in your boat?"

"That's true. I can't argue with that," Deuteronomy conceded.

"Were you and Chess well acquainted?"

"It's a small village. I've lived here all my life."

"Would you say you were friends?"

"No. We were of different generations and temperaments."

"Your housekeeper told us he visited you recently."

"Last fall. He wanted to talk about a writing project he proposed to undertake."

"And what was that?"

"A true crime book about the Cold War. He wanted to know what cases I thought he might include."

"Why would Chess Biederman want to write about the Cold War?"

"Who can say? Based on what little I know of him, he appeared to be a man of eclectic interests—for example, those sex machines or whatever they are that he's been making. Also, he was quite the devotee of popular music and Eastern mysticism, I believe, or at least he once was. It seems he was also interested in the Cold War."

"Why would he consult you?"

"Apparently, you've forgotten that I used to write spy novels," Deuteronomy said, piqued. "My nom de plume was Nash Hammer."

"That's right. I think I knew that."

"I would imagine so," Deuteronomy said in an imperious tone. "How many popular authors live in this village?"

"Did someone tell me one of your books was made into a movie?"

"Several were. There was also a television series. That was more than a few years ago, of course."

"I don't suppose you know of a reason why someone would want to murder Chess?"

"No."

"Just a few more questions. Who had access to the boat?"

"No one that I'm aware of, but it's hard to say precisely. The boat is stored at the back of Ernestine Cutter's land. I suppose almost anyone could have snuck back there without being observed. However, it was shrink-wrapped in the fall— just after Thanksgiving, I believe—and unless you know something I do not, no one's touched it since."

"You haven't visited the boat since last fall?"

"Why would I? You know what Maine winters are like."

"That's all for now. I'll be back in touch if there's anything else. Thank you for your time."

Deuteronomy sat in the parlor for a few minutes after Officer Bernier departed and reflected on Chess's death. Deuteronomy was not a man much given to emotion. He felt a certain sadness at Chess's passing, but it was an acknowledgment of the transient nature of life, not of a sense of personal loss. Yet, curiously, there was something else: a physical response, a pulse, even a sense of elation. Deuteronomy was intrigued by the manner of Chess's passing and, if he were honest with himself, excited by it. He pondered this unexpected and titillating occurrence and what he might do to untangle the mystery. Eventually he rose and went looking for Elektra. He found her reading by the kitchen table.

"What are you reading?"

"The Zane Grey. Is western."

"Why are you reading that?" Deuty asked, baffled, as he often was by Elektra's wide and, in his opinion, undiscerning taste in literature.

"Why not read this? Reading help to improve the English."

"I was reflecting on some costumes my wife and I once kept for costume parties and Halloween," Deuty said. "Have these been discarded, or are they stored away?"

"Why you want the dress-up things? Is not Halloween, and people not invite you to party anymore anyway. You not even go out!"

"That is an exaggeration. I do go out. I am fond of going outside at night in the summer, particularly for rides in my boat."

"What of this? I am the one that steering."

"Who steers is not relevant to how often I go out or where the costumes are," Deuteronomy replied testily.

"You know the dress-up things in attic!" Elektra exclaimed, equally exasperated.

Climbing the stairs, he reflected on how irritating Elektra had become. Surely she hadn't been like this years ago when he hired her, or he never would have. Arriving at the third floor landing, he opened the door to the attic and climbed a shorter series of steps to his final destination.

The attic was rarely visited. It was unfinished. The trusses had been filled with insulation but were exposed, and plywood had been nailed over the floor to create a rudimentary walkway. Although it was large, running half the length of the house, the pitch of the roof greatly reduced the space in which it was possible to stand fully erect.

In spite of these limitations the space had been well used as a dumping ground for that which was no longer immediately useful but was too precious, inconvenient or imbued with sentiment to part with. Taped boxes were stacked four feet high and even higher in the center.

Although the boxes were covered with dust, they were not as dirty as they might have been, given their length of stay. The reason for this was that a year earlier, over Elektra's objections, Deuteronomy had demanded that several neighborhood lads be employed to arrange the boxes sequentially in chronological order from most ancient to most recent and affix labels, neatly printed in permanent ink, describing the contents of each. He also demanded a thorough vacuuming.

He congratulated himself on his foresight in pushing through this important organizational initiative, which would now prove so useful in locating the critical item he sought. He estimated what the approximate antiquity of the costumes might be and calculated a rough location. He was correct within four boxes. There they were, Costumes and Accessories c. 1975.

Deuteronomy deftly ripped off the tape and opened the flaps. Digging through the contents, he remembered that his fourth and most recent wife had convinced him for more than a decade to appear at Halloween parties as Abraham Lincoln to her Mary Todd and, after that, as Samson to her Delilah.

He continued to dig through the box and found New Year's Eve hats and noisemakers. Beneath them, at the bottom of the box, he found what he was looking for—a long bushy beard and mustache that were part of his Samson costume, as well as a tube of theatrical adhesive. This, he quickly realized, had long since dried up. He resealed the box and returned downstairs with the facial hair. The adhesive went into the trash. The disguise went into his bedroom.

As she always did, Elektra served Deuteronomy dinner in his room promptly at 5:00 p.m.

"For boat ride we go tonight?" she asked him after setting the tray down.

"No. I'm tired. I'll be turning in early."

Shortly before dusk he checked to see that Elektra was in her room, watching television. He dressed in dark, casual clothing and attached the facial hair with the only substance he had at hand, rubber cement from his desk drawer. It immediately fell off. After several attempts he concluded he was so rarely seen around the village that he wasn't likely to be recognized with or without biblical facial hair.

It had been quite a while since he had driven his car, but after a hunt he located his keys and a small flashlight. As dusk turned to night he placed these in his pocket, opened a window and slowly climbed out. It wasn't the easiest maneuver. He wasn't as young as he once was, and he wasn't in the most vigorous condition, due to his insufficiency of exercise. Still, he managed it and scurried toward the garage, unnoticed. He started the car and pulled out as slowly as possible, hoping not to attract Elektra's attention.

He headed out of Horeb toward Zion, the county seat. The exact route was somewhat unclear to him. The narrow two-lane road that had always wound through the towns between Horeb and Zion was now wide and four lanes, and it included a new bypass to larger roads that Deuteronomy had never encountered before. He had to stop and ask for directions at a gas station that had mysteriously arisen in a former wild blueberry barren, but he finally drove into Zion and headed for his destination: the county morgue.

Dr. Estes Worthington, who had served as the county medical examiner for decades, had been a close personal friend, offering his extensive knowledge of forensics to assist Deuteronomy in peppering his books with grisly details. Deuteronomy fondly recalled that each year in the spring, the time when death seemed to slow between the end of winter and the arrival of the first tourists, they would have tea almost every afternoon in Estes's office. Deuteronomy was certain that if he wasn't dead himself, Estes would have dissected Chess Biederman chop-chop and conclusively determined what had happened to him.

It was unfortunate that Deuteronomy did not know Estes's replacement—or perhaps by now, Estes's replacement's replacement. But Deuteronomy did know that whoever he was (or given how topsy-turvy the world had become, possibly *she* was), he wouldn't be there at this hour. Further, unless things had changed, the security at the morgue was lax. Surely Deuteronomy could sneak in for a quick peek at Chess's body, through either the main entrance in the basement or one of the back windows.

Deuteronomy parked about a block away from the municipal building and scurried toward the lower door. The street was dark and empty, as streetlights seem to be considered frivolous in Maine, and he was sure he no one had seen him.

Arriving at the door, he was surprised that the bronze nameplate proclaiming "Morgue" was no longer present. A vinyl sign reading "Deliveries" had replaced it.

He tried the door. It was locked. He looked in a few windows but could see very little in the darkened rooms. He tried each of the windows, but these were locked as well. Discouraged, he turned around to head back to his car. Suddenly, he found a uniformed security guard standing in front of him.

"What are you doing?" the guard asked.

"I was ... I was just ..." Deuteronomy stammered, startled. "Where is the morgue?"

"There's no morgue here anymore," the guard answered suspiciously. "They moved it to Augusta years ago. Now what you are you doing here?"

Unable to create a convincing explanation, the police were summoned. Deuteronomy Smelt spent the rest of the night in a jail cell.

Six

The next morning, Cummings went online.

He read up on Wilhelm Reich, the Austrian psychoanalyst considered to be one of the most radical figures in the history of psychiatry. Born in 1897, his ideas on the relationship of the personality and the body influenced many radical therapists who came after him, but his ideas on sexuality made him a figure of increasing controversy. He invented the term *orgone* in the late 1930s to express a universal energy he claimed to have discovered, though in truth it was similar to the *kundalini* proposed in India many centuries earlier. Shortly before World War II, he began building orgone accumulators to provide patients with vehicles for harnessing the presumed health benefits of the orgone.

Eventually his radical ideas landed him in serious trouble. He was imprisoned for fraud in the 1950s. He died of heart failure in 1957 in the United States Penitentiary in Lewisburg, Pennsylvania.

The fact that both Therese and Chess had a connection to Reich, i.e., Therese's biography and Chess's orgone boxes, was intriguing, but it could be just a coincidence. If it was more than that, Cummings needed to discover what the connection was.

Moving on, he searched for background information that might help him understand the Mathers Society. To be specific, he looked at informational and social media sites to see what he could learn about pagan activities in and around

Chicago. He discovered that Chicago Pagan Pride would occur a week hence and made a note to attend it.

Next there was the question of Ida Craddock's leg bone. Why would someone be interested in it? The complexity of human religious experience and the passion with which humans engage in it is never to be underestimated, but Cummings had never heard of pagan reliquaries. Were they as common as relics of the saints? Were they sought after, say, in some kind of black market?

There was no online narrative description of the Craddock Brooch. While there was a brisk international marketplace for all manner of amulets, stones, candles, books, medallions, wands and T-shirts—as one vendor put it, "New Age essentials"—there was very little to be found on the Internet about pagan reliquaries. Yes, an eagle's talon said to have belonged to Cornelius Agrippa, the medieval occultist, hung on a golden chain around the neck of a Tennessee wine merchant. Yes, British magus Aleister Crowley's left testicle was said to be in a display case at the Temple of Thelema in Glendale, California. But compared to the relics of Jesus and his devotees, including the locks of hair, bones, dried organs, fingernail parings, pieces of the true cross and all the rest, the pagans seemed to have left remarkably few *memento mori.*

Cummings had more success in one area: the Craddock Brooch's sale history. By searching an auction database Cummings determined that it had been sold twice during the previous few years, both times by Clarkson's auction house, located on the fringes of downtown Chicago. The prices were not excessively hefty. Bidder CB175 purchased the brooch on March 27, 2006, for $1,150, and bidder CB234 purchased it on June 6, 2009, for $1,250.

That the auction house was physically in Chicago might be no more than a coincidence. Most auctions are now conducted online, and buyers could be anywhere. Still, who the buyers were might be of interest.

Cummings considered ways to get Clarkson's to divulge the confidential names and addresses of the purchasers. He set the timer on his wristwatch and brainstormed possibilities on a legal pad. When the buzzer sounded, he still had no idea which manipulation, if any, might prove most effective, but he had decided to visit Clarkson's nonetheless. Perhaps something would occur to him spontaneously.

Clarkson's turned out to be a dilapidated brick warehouse in a neighborhood lately full of loft conversions and upscale chain stores. It had been refurbished to make it look like a suitable repository for the world's artistic treasures, but paint and exuberance can accomplish only so much. The building sought to be a courtesan but remained a five-dollar hooker.

Cummings entered the red wrought aluminum front gates flanked by reproduction Chinese lions and opened a very ordinary glass door. He proceeded to an even more ordinary reception area, staffed by a young man with elegantly cut green hair.

Cummings hadn't come up with a gambit that was better than weak, but human incompetence being what it is, sometimes weak is enough. He embarked with the first manipulation that came to mind.

"I wonder if you could help me," Cummings began. "I'm a private detective working to help a client establish the provenance of an item recently stolen from his collection. We're trying to build a case to maximize the payment from the insurer. The item was sold here twice during the last few years ..."

"I'm so sorry, sir," the youth interrupted. "Requests for records must be submitted by certified mail and include photocopies of two forms of identification. Also, we'll need a notarized statement from your client, authorizing us to release the documents to you."

"I see," Cummings said. So much for human weakness.

As he considered his next move, Cummings's eyes drifted across the surface of the reception desk. There he saw a flyer announcing upcoming auctions. These had names like July Premiere Auction and Summer Fine Arts Auction.

"Do you sell many occult items?" Cummings asked.

The young man seemed confused. "Do you mean primitive art?"

"No, I mean ..." and then Cummings realized he didn't really know, broadly speaking, what items might qualify as occult. "I mean, for example, the Craddock Brooch. It belonged to Ida Craddock, a woman who talked to angels and wrote sex manuals or something. You sold it twice in the last five years."

"Jewelry," the young man responded.

"Possibly jewelry but with a supernatural twist."

"Perhaps you are referring to next week's Fine Jewelry and Couture Auction. It includes several items that belonged to Emma Hardinge Britten, a famous nineteenth century spiritualist. I believe there is a ball gown, a pocket watch, a cameo, a cloisonné scrying dish and a lingam."

"Yes!" Cummings responded. "When exactly is that auction?"

The young man provided the information, and Cummings entered it into his smartphone. It would be interesting to see who turned up to bid on these items, and perhaps he could somehow also determine who was bidding remotely.

On the drive back he took a route that passed the Red and White, or what was left of it. The building was marked off with yellow tape, informing passersby in bold black letters that the venue was now a crime scene. There were no actual policemen guarding the site.

Cummings parked a block away. He opened his glove compartment and took out a flashlight and latex gloves from the many just-in-case items he always kept there.

He approached the building cautiously, looking around to ensure he wasn't attracting attention. He bent under some police tape and entered through what had been the front window.

The red brick structure remained intact, but the interior was littered with charred detritus: melted fixtures, burnt wood, shattered windows, blackened wiring and piping, and what remained of tables, chairs, banquettes, window treatments, cutlery, glassware and china.

He moved carefully and slowly across the rubble toward the center of the room in a spiral pattern, in keeping with the common crime scene search method. There seemed to be little of interest to him in the room, but eventually he noticed something.

Picking it up, he determined it was a white business size envelope, slightly damp and partially burnt, addressed to Otto Verissimo. Inside, singed but mostly intact, was a handwritten note. Cummings read it. Intrigued by the content, he put it into his pocket. Then he went home and phoned Otto.

Seven

Most visitors to Maine see only its relaxed July face: lighthouses and sea breezes, scrubbed villages and roughhewn gentility. In the main, the state is not July but December: spectacular but remote wilderness, dented double-wide mobile homes, xenophobic villages with irresolvable class divisions, long winters knocking back Allen's Coffee Brandy in shabby ice fishing shacks and tribal reservations where the average life expectancy is less than fifty.

Still, Maine, like many beautiful and complicated places, evokes a strong love of place that cannot be easily explained. Some are born in the state and stay because it's comfortable or because it's uncomfortable but it's home or because they can't afford to leave; some move to Maine by choice, discover it's not their summer fantasy and learn to accept it for what it is. As for the rest, they drink or they go.

Arriving at the Portland Jetport for Chess's funeral, Cummings picked up a rental car and headed north toward Horeb.

While he was driving the forty or so miles between the airport and the village, his cell phone rang.

"Hi, Dad. What's up?"

"I am perplexed, Son. I am working a crossword. The word I need is nine letters. The clue is in the form of a question, 'Vatican rhythm?'"

"Conundrum," Cummings replied without hesitation.

"You always know the answers, Son," George responded. His tone was factual rather than flattering.

"How are you, Dad?" Cummings asked, then added, "And how is Orchid?" referring to his stepmother.

"I am cryptic. She is beauteous. Where are you?"

"I'm in Maine, actually. I just flew in. I'm attending a funeral. I was going to call you to say hello."

"Who died?"

"Nobody you know."

George and Orchid lived in Maine. Orchid had always lived there. After a life in New York City, George had moved to Maine from his Florida retirement after meeting Orchid.

"That is confounding," George responded. "We are in Baltimore at a Scrabble tournament. Did you know the world's first dental school was founded in Baltimore in 1840?"

"No, I didn't, Dad." Cummings was relieved that he wouldn't have to see them. His feelings toward his father were driven by duty rather than affection. As to his stepmother, the truth was that he didn't like her much. "Have fun. Say hello to Orchid. I'll see you on another trip."

"When you come, Orchid will bake a chicken, and we'll do crossword puzzles."

"What did you mean when you said you were cryptic?" Cummings asked.

"'Mysterious or obscure.'"

"I know what the word means. I mean, how does it apply to you?"

"I have sixteen new puzzle books. Sometimes the clues are difficult."

"I see," he said, although he really didn't. "Okay, Dad. I'll talk to you soon."

They disconnected.

Cummings's father was, and his mother had been, decidedly unusual. Many years earlier, at that stage of early adulthood in which some objectivity about one's family sets in, Cummings had realized they both might have some form of undiagnosed autism. This was some intellectual comfort to him but didn't retroactively alter the limitations of his childhood. He had concluded early that his was not the usual child-parent relationship.

"I got beat up," Cummings remembered sobbing to George when he came home one afternoon at the age of seven. He tried to climb into George's lap for comfort, but George pushed him away.

"Son," George said, "can you think of a seven-letter word that starts with *N*? It means horsey."

Cummings looked at George.

"I got beat up," Cummings repeated. George looked back, confused. Looking at George's baffled expression, Cummings suddenly understood: There would be no comfort in this childhood. "Neighed," he responded.

"Very good, Son! Very good!"

Cummings nodded and then walked to the bathroom to tend to his bruises himself.

Matilda, Cummings's mother, was much older than her husband. She was already in her forties when Cummings, her only child, was born. Her torso was as square and dense as a fire hydrant, and she was barely taller than one. Her arms and legs were stubby but strong. She was unimaginative and inarticulate, and she had no interest in good works, housekeeping, nutrition, fashion or child rearing, nor any interest in pretending she did.

What she did have was extraordinary physical precision. As a girl she had been the New Jersey women's fencing champion, junior division. Cummings sometimes came home from kindergarten to discover her parrying with her friend, Beatrice. Typically they did this in their bras and slips after a few midafternoon martinis with the black-and-white television tuned to *The Guiding Light.*

But fencing was not Matilda's only passion, even though she had given Cummings his middle name, Flynn, after Errol. She loved all contact sports, and the more contact, the better.

For two years she'd been in the roller derby. In March of 1937 she was part of a group of skaters on their way from Saint Louis to Cincinnati. Their bus blew a tire, collided with a bridge, rolled over and burst into flames. Although she was one of only three passengers who escaped alive, her legs were seriously burned. It was the end of her sporting career, but her interest in athletics continued.

George and Matilda interacted little. Cummings and Matilda interacted less.

"Learn anything good in school today?" she would sometimes ask when Cummings arrived home.

Unsure what reply she was looking for, he would generally answer, "Hard to tell."

She would nod and say, "School bored the crap out of me."

He would nod back.

When he was ten, she taught Cummings to box, or at least tried to. He wasn't good at it, and he knew she was disappointed. Still, he made a Herculean effort, which may be why she never knocked him out. It was bonding of a sort.

They had only one other notable conversation, on the morning of Cummings's thirteenth birthday. Matilda came into Cummings room and said, "Ask your father about your dick."

He nodded. That was it.

When Cummings was thirty-seven, a bus hit and killed Matilda in front of a Boston hotel. She had gone to Boston to see a hockey game.

Some years after her death George met Orchid while visiting Cummings, who was living in Maine at the time. Cummings considered her an emotionally vacant know-it-all, but she was a good match for George. They both lived in a universe in which the human body ended below the brain. Cummings kept in touch, which mostly meant responding to his father's incessant requests for assistance with word puzzles. Beyond this, he visited when he could.

Horeb, founded 1762, current population 2,612, was never a particularly fortunate place. The village on Merrymeeting Bay has grown in the last twenty years. It recently exceeded its previous population peak — 2,382 — achieved in 1850 as a result of Maine's then-thriving seafaring economy.

The Civil War, in which two hundred thirty-seven Horeb men served and more than thirty died, as well as changes in the shipping industry, eroded the town's fortunes. During the latter part of the nineteenth century, the town became again what it was originally, a small, agricultural community. It lost more than a third of its population by 1900. Major fires in 1902 and 1904 destroyed what was left of Horeb's two blocks of downtown.

In 1910, with local dignitaries, one of Maine's U.S. senators and the marching band from the Maine Maritime Academy in attendance, the final ship built in Horeb was launched. As the procession moved toward the water, the ship fell off of its launching platform, skidded down Massachusetts Street and broke in half on the banks of the Carlisle River.

In the 1960s Horeb changed from a stolid farming community to a hippie carnival. In the years since the town had regained balance. Still, Horeb continued to be a rather eccentric place. It was now home to an array of cottage industries: weaving, soap making, organic lamb, pottery, heirloom vegetables and handmade Windsor chairs. There was a town arts center that held exhibits of local painters and sculptors and housed an avant-garde theater company. Next to it was an even more renegade establishment, the Maine Ephemera Museum. The Museum sponsored periodic exhibits of toothbrushes, paper clips, painted flowerpots and other detritus, and it had a permanent collection of umbrella covers from around the world.

The town's location at the approximate midpoint between three prominent towns — Augusta, Maine's capital; Portland, the state's largest city; and Lewiston-Auburn, the state's second largest urban area, known with geographic hubris as L.A.) — helped Horeb to reinvent itself as a small bedroom community. Horeb's residents were dispersed among thirty-four square miles of woods and farms, and former woods and farms, inland from the village proper. The population of the village itself was about two hundred fifty. Its main road, Massachusetts Street, ran about two miles from the Horeb exit on I-295 until it dead-ended into Water Road, otherwise known as Route 240, a small state highway. In between there were a handful of streets that ran perpendicular or parallel to Massachusetts. There were perhaps six streets in all. Horeb had one traffic light — flashing yellow only — a gas station, a diner and a small market.

There were no commercial lodgings in Horeb, though there were bed-and-breakfasts in several nearby villages. Cummings had an open invitation to stay with Ernestine.

As he drove into the village, Cummings was surprised to discover that he felt a certain odd attachment to the place. He assumed this reflected his feelings for Ernestine rather than his love for Horeb.

Ernestine lived in a Greek Revival house built in 1835. It had four Doric columns, double-hung, twelve-sash windows, and square openings for windows and doors adorned with acanthus medallions. The house had been tastefully updated with modern technologies, but it was architecturally intact down to its still-functional beehive oven and a hidden room to hide slaves escaping on the Underground Railroad. Ernestine kept it painted it a historically incorrect gray (instead of white) with lavender shutters (rather than black). Cummings wondered if the house reflected both Ernestine's attachment to, and rebellion against, her lineage.

Ernestine was of medium height and always had her white hair pulled back in a simple bun. Though her choice of words often seemed anachronistic, and her expansive, eighteenth-century home could have been a museum, her dress was modern and casual. She dressed simply and comfortably, usually in a flannel shirt, jeans and boots from L.L. Bean.

Ernestine's housekeeper, Rebecca — a pleasant, stout older woman who spoke in a Downeast accent even more pronounced than Ernestine's — helped Cummings put his suitcases into one of Ernestine's guest rooms. Then she made a pot of tea, and Ernestine and Cummings sat down to talk.

"She's such a dear," Ernestine said, referring to Rebecca. "I didn't know what I'd do when Becky left last year to live with her sons in Tallahassee. You remember Becky?"

Cummings nodded. He'd been fond of Ernestine's former housekeeper.

"It was good of you to come," Ernestine said, changing the subject to the reason for Cummings's trip.

"I liked Chess. He was very eccentric, but so many people in Maine are."

"Is Maine so different from other places?" Ernestine countered. "Life makes many folks half mad in one way or another, sometimes three-quarters."

"That's true," Cummings conceded. "Anyway, the trip gives me a chance to see you."

Ernestine dismissed the implied affection with a half-smile and a slight shake of her head. "But mostly to investigate," she said.

"Was there anything of note you didn't tell me on the phone? Anything you might have observed when you saw the body?"

"No, I don't believe so."

"What about Chess's life? Anything notable there?"

"You do know his business rose like a rocket a few years back?"

"What business? Do you mean the orgone boxes?"

"Yes, indeed. You remember that his previous business ventures failed? For instance, there was the time he came back from a trip to the South Seas and started manufacturing Polynesian clothes. It was a disaster. As one local wag said, 'puce sarongs do not make a right.' Anyway, Chess put those orgone boxes on the computer, and orders began coming from all over, not just the United States but Europe, Asia, South America. He had to move the manufacturing out of his garage and into that old building by the river that nobody's used since Sally Fishmeyer made Ho Chi Minh T-shirts during the Vietnam War. Fixing up that building and paying rent to the Village, as well as creating a bunch of new jobs, made him wicked popular. I cannot imagine anybody would want to kill him. I cannot imagine it."

The next day, Cummings, in a dark suit and tie, and Ernestine, in her grandmother's wedding dress which she'd had dyed black many years earlier for just such occasions, drove the ten miles to the First Congregational Church in Samaria. There, a properly somber service was held, followed by an interment in the churchyard and a reception in the church basement.

Like most Congregational churches in Maine — indeed, like Maine itself — the building was Federal and stolid. Its weathered clapboards reminded one that Maine existed in a long trajectory of time. Everything had been seen before.

First Congregational was the oldest church in the area. The sanctuary was built in 1793 and subsequently renovated and enlarged several times. There were presently three buildings: the church proper, the parish hall and the rectory.

At the reception Cummings saw almost everyone he knew in Horeb. This reminded him of how colorful Horeb actually was. By comparison Chicago seemed as unimaginative as corn.

Feenie Malaga greeted him. She was a performance artist named for phenobarbital by her besotted mother because "you know what they say about Maine, mostly drinking villages with small fishing problems." She had violent violet hair and a contorted chrysanthemum tattoo on her arm. Cummings had originally encountered her in a local supermarket, buying a quart of vodka, a quart of milk and a quart of Drano, which had led him to wonder briefly if this was some kind of local mixed drink.

Her brother Isidore, who rarely said anything but was noted for his paintings of pigeons, was also there. As usual, he was austerely dressed in a black suit, black tie, white shirt, white socks and black shoes. The only burst of color on him was his hair, which was a shade of pumpkin.

Cassandra Parsons, the proprietress of the Horeb Country Store, nodded at Cummings as he passed by. She was a study in brusqueness: tall and thin but more than that, angular. Her face was tanned and worn. Her nails were short, and so was her piebald grey and brown hair. Her facial expression, to the extent that she had one, was a half-frown. Her cheerfully rude teenager daughter, Alice, was with her. Alice gave Cummings the finger and smiled.

He saw his former boss, Birdie Wordsworth, the benefactress of the Panegyricus Foundation, an arts philanthropy that gave money to creative individuals to "promote the ineffable visions of the individual." At her Florida residence, using only a luncheon fork, she had once saved her gardener from a python.

Norbert and Glenda Auchincloss waved at Cummings from across the room. They owned a nudist sauna but today were dressed in dark summer weight wool. Glenda, a small, bulky creature who looked like an anthropomorphic potato, was deaf and originally from California. There she'd taken up S&M. Highly flexible, if not very affable, she was known by her friends as "the wicked switch of the West."

Moving on from the parade of individualists, Cummings spoke with Chess's father, Fletcher, Horeb's postmaster, who was as devastated by the loss of his son as one would expect. Cummings offered his condolences.

Finally Cummings saw Officer Bernier sitting in a window seat, working on a piece of lace shaped like a moose head. Cummings realized he had never seen Officer Bernier out of uniform.

"How are you, Officer Bernier?"

Bernier, who didn't remember Cummings, stared for a moment, trying to identify him. When he did, he scowled slightly.

"Mister Wanamaker. I thought you'd moved to the Midwest."

"I have. I came back for Chess's funeral. A very sad day."

"I trust you won't be interfering with any of my investigations while you're here?"

"When have I ever interfered, Officer Bernier?" Cummings smiled.

"When have you indeed?" Bernier scowled again.

Apparently, he hadn't forgiven Cummings for solving several cases that Bernier couldn't solve himself while he lived in the village.

Cummings returned to Ernestine, who was sipping fruit punch to which she had added brandy from a sterling silver flash hidden in her décolletage.

"Is Smelt here? Or his housekeeper?" Cummings asked, surveying the room.

"I haven't seen them, dear," Ernestine said, "but that is not a surprise. I think I told you that Deuty keeps very much to himself. As to Elektra, she works for Deuty, but she's never really been part of the community."

"Perhaps I should pay them a visit. Elektra found the body, didn't she?"

"I'm not sure how effective a visit might be. Deuty can be irascible."

"Perhaps if you call ahead and grease the wheels for me."

"Oh, that won't do any good. Deuty doesn't use the telephone. He writes postcards."

"I don't understand."

"If he has something to say, he writes it down on a postcard and has Elektra mail it or hand it along to somebody. It's just his way, dear."

On the drive back from the church, Cummings convinced Ernestine that giving him an introduction to Deuteronomy Smelt was worth a try. So she wrote a note on Cummings's behalf, stating he'd be dropping by the following day. They walked to the Smelt house and slipped it under the door. On the walk back she told Cummings what she knew of Deuteronomy and his household.

"Deuteronomy had an aunt, Cornelia Smelt Paddington. She died many years ago and left him money and his house. I believe he lives off of those funds plus whatever he may have saved from his glory days. His books don't sell well — at least, not anymore. He wrote a lot of spy novels under the name of Nash Hammer. Did I tell you that?"

"Yes, I think you did."

"I don't believe he's written a new book in, oh, it must be years and years now. The end of the Cold War took the wind out of him. He enjoyed the Cold War more than most folks. I don't believe he much likes anything that has happened since, but that sort of attitude isn't uncommon here. My grandfather used to say that nothing of consequence had happened in Maine since the Civil War."

"What about the housekeeper?"

"Oh, Elektra's lived in his house for decades. They say she came to Boston from Greece to marry a Greek immigrant she met through a lonely hearts advertisement. I hear the marriage turned out more *House of Atreus* than *House and Garden,* if you know what I mean. The husband died of a heart attack many years ago, and she moved to Maine to work in a hotel. Then she met Deuty and his wife, Edwina, and Elektra went to work for them. Edwina passed on a year ago, but Elektra's still there, just as always."

"Do you think there's something between them?"

"Deuty and Elektra? You know we don't ask that sort of question northwards of Boston," Ernestine said playfully, "but I suspect the answer would be no. They don't seem suited to each other in that way."

Elektra answered the door after Cummings knocked several times. Apparently the doorbell was not working, an element of disrepair that seemed consistent with the house's faded and peeling exterior paint.

"Hello. I'm Cummings Flynn Wanamaker."

"I am the Elektra Philemon, the lady that finds the body. Animals eat on this body. Also this body freeze and thaw, freeze and thaw, freeze and thaw. Looks like the head of the doll made from the dried apple but with the fruit missing," Elektra explained. "What else you want to know?"

"Would it be possible to speak to Mister Smelt?"

"Mister Deuty, he not like people to talk to him. Also Mister Deuty in bad mood. He been arrested."

"For what?"

"Mister Deuty, he try to go someplace that is not good to go."

"I believe Ernestine Cutter wrote a note of introduction to Mister Smelt on my behalf."

"Oh! I am knowing of this note. Mister Deuty he say he like to talk to you. You come in and on the sofa in the parlor I put you."

Cummings walked into the front hallway. It reminded him somewhat of Otto's home: wooden, dark and oppressive. However, someone with taste had built this home. Although the interior was worn and faded — the wallpaper looked like it had been put up more than a hundred years earlier — all surfaces were spotlessly clean. Evidently Elektra took her duties very seriously.

Elektra escorted Cummings to the parlor where he sank into an overstuffed, threadbare settee. She then walked down the hall and stopped in front of a heavy maple door. "Mister Deuty, the visitor to you is now on the sofa," she said, knocking gently. There was no response. She knocked again. "Mister Deuty?" Again there was no response.

Elektra sighed with mild irritation and picked up a postcard from the random assortment piled on a table by the door. The card was from the 1950s and read, "Greetings from Rehoboth Beach." She took a pen from her pocket, wrote a brief note in her fractured English, explaining that a guest had arrived, and slipped it under the door. She waited. A few moments later, to her great surprise, the door opened.

"Is he in the parlor?"

"Yes, Mister Deuty," she said.

Deuteronomy entered the room with his hand extended. His voice conveyed something like friendliness. "Hello, young man."

"Thank you for seeing me. I'm Cummings Flynn Wanamaker. I believe you know that I'm a friend of Ernestine's. I used to live in Horeb. Honestly, I'm surprised we didn't meet while I lived in the village. It's such a small place."

"You've undoubtedly heard that I'm a recluse. Truth be told, most people aren't worth one's time. That said, Ernestine speaks very highly of you, and I have my concerns about the competence of the local constabulary."

"A concern Ernestine and I share," Cummings said, reflecting on the incompetence of Officer Bernier, who had failed to solve his late partner Terry's murder.

"So I understand," Deuteronomy continued. "Also, frankly, I had a minor scrape with the law last week which reminded me that I am too old to do what I once did. Thus, for all of these reasons, I thought we might work together."

"Work together?"

"Of course. You don't think I'd wish to speak to you just for conversation? I believe that Chess Biederman's death needs to be investigated."

"As do I," Cummings concurred.

"Very well. I'm going to provide you with the information I have, which is not much, I'm afraid. Then I hope you will proceed from there and let me know, from time to time, how things are progressing."

"Do you have a special interest in this?"

"I knew Chess, of course, but the truth is, I'm just intrigued. This case breaks my routine to which, I fear, I have succumbed over the years. Now then, let me tell you what I know."

Deuteronomy repeated what he'd told Officer Bernier about Chess, adding more minor details, such as an expanded discussion of his conversation with Chess about his Cold War book. He then sent Cummings on his way.

Cummings waited until dark and then strode with a flashlight across Ernestine's property. He found the boat which, along with the surrounding area, had been neatly taped off as a crime scene. Cummings climbed under the tape and focused his flashlight on the boat. The shrink-wrap was gone. He saw several large scratches on one side of the vessel. Their cause was unclear.

Cummings climbed onto the boat and moved slowly across the deck, perusing it carefully. In the small front cabin there were curious dried, brownish discolorations; presumably, this is where Chess's body lay through the winter, and the discolorations were from bodily fluids.

Next Cummings walked to the small section of the village on the shore of the Carlisle River. He cautiously approached his destination, an old brick warehouse, making sure he wasn't observed.

As a sign indicated, the building was the current home of BEIDERMAN ORGONE BOXES, LLC. As he anticipated, the main door was locked. However, Cummings was pleased to discover that several side windows had not been. He pried one open and hoisted himself inside. This process was assisted on the descent by a large oak worktable that had been pushed against a wall directly under the window.

He moved the beam of his flashlight around the space and saw that it wouldn't be difficult to explore. It was oblong and open, measuring perhaps three thousand square feet. It had been set up as a woodworking shop with a variety of machines and tools neatly organized in various workstations around the periphery. At one end there were several doors. Exploring further, he found that these were restrooms and a lunchroom, all unlocked. He easily jimmied open the one locked door he discovered with a credit card. This turned out to be an office. Presumably, as the owner of the business, it belonged to Chess.

Inside there was a desk, a desk chair, a small conference table with chairs and several filing cabinets. The room was in a disjointed state, part order and part chaos.

The orderly section centered on the desk onto which documents and files had been neatly piled. Upon closer inspection Cummings determined that these were materials relating to the business, such as invoices, shipping receipts and personnel records.

The remaining items, which appeared to be personal, had been dumped with little thought onto the conference table. Apparently someone was running the business in Chess's absence and had simply pushed the nonessential materials aside.

The personal items included holiday and birthday cards inscribed to Chess, a hand-knitted ski cap and matching scarf, a half-eaten box of chocolates, a large holiday gift basket from which many items had been removed, and personal papers, some in files and some scattered haphazardly. These personal papers included a newspaper account of a presentation by Chess to the Sagadahoc County Chamber of Commerce, insurance paperwork, photocopies of articles about Wilhelm Reich, two seed catalogs and an unanswered wedding invitation. Cummings looked at this and didn't recognize the name of the bride or the groom.

Eventually Cummings found a file that contained Chess's notes on the Cold War book, including the handwritten notes Chess had made on a legal pad when he and Deuteronomy met to discuss the project. Reading through them, he observed that the notes seemed to reflect the conversation between Deuteronomy and Chess as Deuteronomy had described it to Cummings. There was also a two-page handwritten list of the cases Chess planned to write about. Cummings scanned this, but as he had no knowledge of Cold War espionage, it had no meaning to him. He tucked it under his arm to show to Deuteronomy along with the Chamber of Commerce article.

Cummings carefully climbed back out through the window and closed it. Then he walked back to Ernestine's house, dropped the papers by his bed and went back out for some additional nighttime snooping.

As he approached Chess's house, which was only a quarter-mile or so from Ernestine's, Cummings saw that it was a white paper plate of a place, a typical 1950s ranch house. To the left of the house Cummings observed a straight driveway plodding from the street to an attached garage. An old MG convertible, dented and discolored, rested like a beaten prizefighter on the asphalt.

Seeing no one, Cummings moved closer to the front of the house. There were two doors: a metal and glass outer door with a wooden door inside. Small bay windows framed the doors on either side. A low hedge of closely planted euonymus in need of a trim framed the facade. Between the hedge and the street there was lawn.

Cummings opened the outer door and looked at the hinges, the glass pane and the metal casing. Nothing seemed noteworthy. He tried the handle of the inner door. It was locked.

He went to the back door. To Cummings's surprise, it was unlocked. Inside, he found himself in a mudroom, the transitional space in New England houses between winter and warmth. The accumulation of dust suggested that no one had been in the house in months. As is typically the case, the mudroom was little more than a place to take off one's snow boots and heavy coat. On the far wall there was a door to the rest of the house. To the right there was a wall of coat hooks and beneath them, a low bench. To the left there was a wall adorned with photographs and a door, presumably to the garage.

Cummings looked at the photos. They seemed to be family pictures: ball games, dance recitals, lobster bakes. He recognized Chess and his father in many of them. He recognized much younger versions of Deuteronomy and Ernestine in the background of several.

Hanging beside the photographs was a hand-calligraphed Biederman genealogical chart with information going back to the 1600s. An inscription informed Cummings that this was a gift to a woman, perhaps Chess's mother, on her sixtieth birthday. Cummings studied the photographs and the genealogical chart but saw nothing illuminating.

Cummings went into the garage. There he found a small desk, benches, saw horses, hand tools, power tools, lumber and hardware, all organized neatly on shelves and pegboard.

Cummings noticed plans for an orgone accumulator tacked onto the garage wall above the desk.

He glanced down to the surface of the desk. It was cluttered with loose papers. One caught his attention: a "to do" list. Cummings picked it up. It noted errands, phone calls, bills that were due. One item struck Cummings as being of possible interest. It read "consolidation loan?" Was this a routine financial transaction, or was Chess in financial trouble, and could that have had something to do with his death? Cummings looked for financial statements but found none.

Returning to the mudroom, Cummings entered the living room and then went up the stairs. He sneezed and coughed. He was disturbing settled dust by moving through the house, and it was beginning to irritate his respiratory tract. He wished he'd thought to bring a protective mask.

Upstairs he found three bedrooms and a bathroom. Two bedrooms were empty. In the third he found a bed, a dresser, a nightstand with an alarm clock, a lamp and a closet full of men's clothes, presumably Chess's. Cummings looked quickly through the closet and in the dresser and nightstand drawers, but he found nothing of interest.

The bathroom was similarly uninteresting: soap, shaving cream, a razor, a toothbrush, toothpaste, deodorant and an expired bottle of acetaminophen.

He went downstairs to the kitchen. This was a small room that, like so many American kitchens of a certain age, had a tone of enforced cheerfulness: It was painted a shade of yellow so overweening that the dark half of the day seemed to be no more than an astronomical faux pas.

There was a breakfast nook with a small wooden table and two rattan chairs, each bursting with a sunflower seat cushion. On the wall above was a portrait of a man standing beside what appeared to be a giant Flash Gordon ray gun. Looking closer, Cummings read a caption identifying the man as Wilhelm Reich and the contraption's purpose as the accumulation of orgone energy to attract rain.

Cummings moved his gaze to the appliances. They were old but so brightly white they might have had cosmetic dentistry. There were few appliances on the counters and no decorative objects. A small bookshelf hung on one wall. It contained works on cooking and nutrition, notably a number of volumes by Adele Davis, whom Cummings vaguely recalled as an early health food enthusiast.

He opened each drawer and cabinet and carefully searched the contents. He found an assortment of measuring cups, wooden spoons, garlic presses and the like — but nothing that seemed out of place in a kitchen.

He opened the refrigerator door. Although there wasn't much in the refrigerator, what was there resembled a toxic waste dump. Cummings repressed his revulsion and checked through the existing items: a mass that may have once been bread, jars of condiments, two containers of unopened half-and-half and a partially eaten package of moldy feta cheese.

He noted that the dairy products came from a local producer, Omurtag Farm.

Had Deuteronomy mentioned an allergy to dairy products as one of Chess's childhood maladies? He couldn't remember. Even if Deuteronomy had, could it have cleared as Chess had grown up? Alternatively, might Chess keep items such as feta cheese for a girlfriend or other visitors?

In the morning Cummings phoned Deuteronomy's house, but no one answered the phone. He also called Rockland. He confirmed that childhood allergies can recede as children grow up, but they don't always.

It was only a hunch, and one that Cummings expected would lead to nothing, but good investigation requires leaving no details unexplored. For this reason Cummings went to Omurtag Farm after breakfast. It was located on the edge of Horeb. Its brightly painted sign, hung over a large iron gate flanked by old stone walls, announced that it was both "organic and biodynamic." Cummings had some sense of what "organic" meant but had no idea what a "biodynamic" farm might be. He looked up both words on his smartphone. As he suspected, "organic" referred to a lack of use of pesticides. "Biodynamic" referred to a holistic approach to agriculture, which Cummings took to mean a consideration of actions and outcomes. For example, chemicals applied to kill weeds in the fields might have an impact on the cows that grazed nearby.

The gate was open, and Cummings drove through. He continued down a winding dirt road, arriving in about half a mile at a series of connected, whitewashed buildings in a little house/big house/back house/barn configuration. This was a common way in which New England farm buildings were expanded over time. It promoted efficiency by connecting the buildings together to allow for access while protecting their inhabitants, human and nonhuman, from the region's severe winters.

Cummings parked near the barn and got out. He saw a young woman feeding chickens in a large enclosure and approached her.

"I wonder if you can help me? I'm here to make an inquiry about someone who may have purchased dairy products."

"You'll need to talk to Anastas. He should be in the barn." She pointed to a large outbuilding a few acres away.

Inside the barn Cummings found a swarthy man of middling age and height. He wore a T-shirt that read "Horeb — black fly capital of the world" and had shoulder-length salt-and-pepper hair and an unkempt beard that descended to his stomach.

"Are you Anastas?"

"Yes," he said with a significant accent that was difficult to identify.

"I'm Cummings Flynn Wanamaker. I don't believe we've met. I lived in Horeb for a few years."

"I see."

"Have you lived here long? I can't place your accent."

"Bulgaria."

"Really? How did you end up in New England?"

"I fall in love with *Moby Dick,* then I find out nobody hunts the whales no more. Meanwhile I emigrate."

"I see," Cummings continued. "I'm here to ask about one of your customers. Do you remember a man named Chess Biederman? Here's his picture," he said, displaying the image in the newspaper article he'd found in Chess's office.

"I know this name. Why is this?"

"He's dead. His body was discovered a few days ago."

"Why do you ask about this man? He did not die from our cheese."

"I don't believe so, although if he had it would have been a *feta accompli*," Cummings said, unable to restrain himself. "I'm simply trying to learn all I can about him."

Anastas thought for a moment. "I do not recall him. You can ask my wife."

"Where would I find her?"

"We have little store in front. I take you."

They walked to the main building and went in through a side door. Inside, in what was once a barn, there were refrigerator and freezer cases of products for sale along with bins of seasonal vegetables. Cummings glanced inside one of the cases and found several varieties of cheese.

A woman who looked remarkably similar to Anastas, except that she lacked a beard, sat on a stool beside a cash register.

"Galina," Anastas said, "this man is here about man found dead."

"Do you remember Chess Biederman?" Cummings asked her. He showed her the newspaper photograph.

"Yes, I know him. He is here once or twice. He come to buy our milk and cheese for party for his workers. Big order. Last fall, I think." Galina replied. "This is also what I tell the other man."

"Someone else was here asking about Chess?"

"Yesterday. From the police."

"Thank you for your time," Cummings said, moving toward the door. Before he could reach it, it opened.

A tall, thin man came in. He was in his sixties, had bright white hair, a wildly tie-dyed T-shirt, a wilder beard that descended in chaotic straggles to below his belt, and pink and white striped sunglasses. He was Howard Oliver, a local artist and proprietor of the Maine Ephemera Museum. Cummings had met him once or twice during his time in Horeb, but he was sure that Howard Oliver wouldn't remember him.

"Cummings," Howard said with some surprise, "how nice to see you! I thought you'd moved away."

"Good morning, Howard," Cummings responded, impressed by Howard's memory. "It's nice to see you."

"Anastas. Galina. Don't you look well!" Howard said, greeting them. "I was thrilled that you phoned!"

"I get what you come for," Galina said, disappearing into another room. Moments later she reappeared with three umbrellas. These were covered in the usual Stalinist color palette: drab and dingy. She handed them to Howard and said with pride, "My sister send these from Romania just to put in the museum."

"What a gift! What a gift!" Howard effused, taking the objects. "Along with the umbrellas your brother sent from Russia, Ukraine and Georgia, and your other sister sent from Bulgaria, our Eastern European umbrella cover collection will be world class!"

Overhearing this, Cummings imagined Ernestine rolling her eyes at the very idea that umbrella covers were worth collecting, but of course she was not the sort of woman who would be so rude as to roll her eyes.

In the afternoon Cummings returned to Deuteronomy's house and reported on his activities.

"I'm not sure I learned very much that's useful. There were some odd scratches on the side of the boat."

"Odd in what way?"

"They were large and perhaps a quarter of an inch deep. It was difficult to imagine what might have caused them."

"They could be the result of Elektra's steering," Deuteronomy suggested. "I regret that we occasionally become intimate with the rocky coastline of Maine."

"That's possible," Cummings agreed. "Other than that, I found some personal papers I think you'll want to see." He handed the list to Deuteronomy. He skimmed it.

"This reflects our discussion last fall, although he's added a few cases I didn't mention. None of them are obscure, just some additional much-heralded KGB antics."

"I see," Cummings responded. "There's also one other matter. Honestly, I don't know if it's significant or not. I found some dairy products in Chess's refrigerator. I couldn't recall if you said he was allergic to cow's milk."

"I didn't say. I don't know."

"In any case, they came from a local dairy, Omurtag Farm. I went over there and asked if they knew Chess. They remembered he had purchased items for a party for his employees; they remembered it because it was a big order. So even if he was lactose intolerant, that explains why leftovers might have been in his kitchen.

"I was going to follow up with a few additional questions, but I didn't get the chance. Howard Oliver showed up, collecting umbrella covers for his museum. The owners of Omurtag Farm are from Eastern Europe, and apparently relatives from the former Soviet Bloc have been sending them over."

Cummings said this humorously, assuming Deuteronomy thought the Ephemera Museum was as silly as he did. But Deuteronomy responded in a serious, even grave, tone.

"Did they specify where in Eastern Europe?" he asked, picking up Chess's notes for his book.

"Let's see. Romania, Bulgaria, Russia and perhaps several other countries."

Suddenly, still holding Chess's list, Deuteronomy rose. He walked quickly toward his room.

"Is something the matter?" Cummings asked.

"I have to check a few files. I'm not as organized as I once was. This may take some time. I'll telephone you."

"I'm only in Maine until tomorrow."

"I understand. Go now. Go!"

Elektra showed Cummings out.

Eight

Odin, who was not normally gloomy, seemed sullen when he picked up Cummings at the airport.

"Is something wrong?" Cummings asked finally after several minutes of silence.

"I didn't want to tell you on the phone."

"Tell me what?"

"Business travel is down. Multiverse Air is cutting back. Jim called me into his office today and told me I'm being laid off. I don't know what we're going to do."

"Don't worry. We'll manage."

"I don't see how. You're barely making any money, and they're offering a severance package of only six weeks' salary."

"I'm looking for a job and consulting work."

"But you're not finding anything."

"That could change. Anyway, if we have to, we can take money out of our retirement savings."

"Then what will we retire on?"

"I have no idea, but look at the positive. After this recession no one's going to be able to afford to retire ever again!"

Cummings said this in an attempt to lighten the mood, but Odin didn't laugh or even smile.

"That was a joke," Cummings said. Then, trying to sound reassuring, he added, "We'll figure something out."

Chicago Pagan Pride was always held on a Sunday at an Arts and Crafts mansion, Caldecott House, in the suburb of Oak Park. Caldecott House was designed by one of Frank Lloyd Wright's students as a private residence for a wealthy grain merchant and his family. During the Depression a downturn in family fortunes resulted in an accumulation of unpaid real estate taxes. The town of Oak Park acquired the building just before World War II. It was expensive to maintain. To keep the wolf from the ornately carved oak doors, it was regularly rented out for receptions and events, including Pagan Pride.

Cummings stopped at the registration area and picked up a program of the day's events. Workshops would be presented on investigating ghosts, ritual practice, divination techniques, assorted magickal traditions (spelled with a *k* to differentiate it from stage magic) and various pagan religious paths. To Cummings, this was an entirely new world.

The house sat on a large grassy lot, where rings of vendor booths had been arrayed. Most were informal affairs with plastic tables inside simple tenting.

Cummings strolled among the vendor booths and assessed the crowd. The attendees seemed commonplace, if drawn to exotic hair tints, kilts, capes and heavy black eye make-up.

The vendors seemed to represent a mix of pagan sub-genres. These included vodou and hoodoo, which Cummings learned were not the same thing. (The former is a religion, while the latter is a folk magic tradition.) There were Asatru (practitioners of the Nordic traditions); Tarot card readers (which originated in Italy); Traditional Witchcraft devotees (known as "Trad Craft") and many others. The goods for sale included amulets, talismans, crystals, candles, wands, swords, cards, books and even pagan holiday guest towels. Perusing these, Cummings learned Halloween could be referred to by its Celtic name, Samhain, pronounced SOW-in. Cummings also saw blank journals, mystical paintings, ritual clothing such as might be suitable to dress the witches in *Macbeth* and many items designed to interest cats, although there was nothing for dogs.

Cummings attempted to engage vendors in conversation, but his lack of content knowledge made it apparent he was an outsider. Further, his attempts to probe, such as by asking, "What is it you find engaging about all of this?" didn't seem to result in meaningful responses. Instead he received friendly but cold smiles, or nervous giggles, or piercing looks that informed him he'd violated etiquette.

He concluded there was nothing much to see and little more to learn, so he did not stay long. As he left he pondered why mystical leftovers from earlier times continued to be so appealing. An engagement with the supernatural was understandable in the centuries before the triumphs of the rational mind, but what was the fascination of the superstitious now? Wasn't the universe, as understood empirically, mysterious enough?

The next morning, Odin went off at his usual time in order to be at the unemployment office when it opened. Cummings got up early to make Odin breakfast. It didn't improve Odin's mood, but at least he was sent into the world with a full stomach.

Cummings was washing the dishes when there was a polite but firm knock at the front door. One of Chicago's finest flashed his badge and introduced himself as Officer Arnold Bailey.

"You're Cummings Flynn Wanamaker, right?"

"Right."

"May I come in? I'd like to talk to you about the Hickok death."

"Certainly," Cummings said, directing the visitor to the sofa. "You're investigating it as a murder?"

"I know your name. You're that detective guy I read about in the paper, aren't you?"

"Yes."

"Then you should know I can't answer that question. I understand Ms. Hickok was speaking to a group called the Mathers Society when the fire broke out. How long have you been a member?"

"I'm not a member. I've never attended a meeting before. I came with a friend, Luther Bannockburn. He wanted to attend out of curiosity. Also, he teaches music at a local college. Someone who gives a lot of money to his department is a member of the Society. Her name is Anunciación Hollingberry."

"Right," Officer Bailey responded, implying he was familiar with the name. "Could you spell your friend's name?"

Cummings did. Officer Bailey asked for Luther's contact information, which Cummings provided.

"Did you know the deceased?"

"No."

"Never met her before?"

"Never."

"What about a man named Otto Verissimo?"

"I know him."

"How do you happen to know him?"

"He's asked me to speak to him. He has some concerns about Ms. Hickok's death."

"Just so I'm clear, you're an amateur, not a licensed private detective, right?"

"Right."

"I assume you know you can't become a licensed private detective in this state unless you've worked in law enforcement?"

"I've been meaning to research the requirements. I haven't lived in the state very long," Cummings said.

"Just make sure you keep it informal, and don't get in our business. Thank you for your time." Officer Bailey handed Cummings his business card and headed for the door. "That's all for now. We'll be in touch if anything comes up."

As soon as Officer Bailey was gone, Cummings located online the statutes governing private detectives in Illinois. Officer Bailey was correct. If he pursued investigation in Illinois, he would have to remain an amateur.

Cummings turned his attention to the making of money, a topic of escalating importance in view of Odin's loss of a job. He made a few networking phone calls to contacts of contacts, and then he sent his résumé to fifteen additional headhunters, something he was now doing within one hundred miles of Chicago, rather than the fifty-mile radius he had established the previous month.

Sometime later the front door buzzer buzzed "shave and a haircut, two bits." Cummings found this irritating. Opening the door, he found Otto in a tailored English suit with a huge bouquet of flowers. Mandrake, at his side, snapped photos.

"It's such a relief to see you again!" Otto said, handing Cummings the bouquet.

"Thank you, but what's this for?"

"It's an apology for my rudeness in abruptly terminating our last conversation. It's also my way of letting you know that I'm happy you phoned. I really do need your services."

"Come in, please," Cummings said. "I'm sorry we couldn't find a time to meet again sooner. I had to go out of town for a funeral."

"I am sorry for your loss."

"No need to be. It wasn't anyone close. Please sit down. You, too, Mandrake. I could make some tea."

"Don't trouble yourself. It's only us," Otto said. He sat on the sofa. Cummings sat near him. Mandrake sat to the side on an ottoman.

"Why don't you start by telling me why you threw me out so abruptly the last time we met?" Cummings asked.

"You are direct, aren't you?" Otto said.

"Yes," Cummings said.

"I'm afraid my ability to schedule isn't what it should be."

"Anything else?"

"It is possible I may not have told all there is to tell."

"I've already determined that," Cummings responded.

"Have you? You see, you're exactly what I need. Please help me. I'll pay you your usual fee."

"Do you mean help you search for the Craddock Brooch?" Cummings asked.

Mandrake said something unintelligible.

"Oh, dear, Mandrake tells me we must leave now, or we'll be late for Beatrice."

"I thought we were going to talk."

"We are. In the car."

"Where are we going?"

"Here and there. Appointments. Errands. I couldn't cancel. You see? Efficiency. Accomplishing multiple tasks at the same time."

Cummings did not wish to go, but in view of the mention of money he felt he had little choice. He owed it to his household finances.

"Who's Beatrice?" Cummings asked.

"'O lady who causes my hope to have life ...'" Otto replied, quoting the *Divine Comedy* as he led Cummings to the street.

There, they got into the back seat of a very old and very large Rolls Royce. Mandrake put a chauffeur's cap over his yarmulke and climbed into the driver's seat. He pulled away from the curb recklessly and surged down the street with the thrust of a derecho.

Otto kept up a steady chat about this and that. They drove for some time into the outer reaches of suburban Chicago. Cummings did his best to breathe evenly and not fearfully clutch the armrest in response to Mandrake's driving.

"Let's discuss business, shall we? I'll be happy to work with you as a consultant," Cummings said finally, interrupting Otto's stream of small talk. "I'm not a licensed investigator. I am merely providing informal, personal consulting services. You may pay me an honorarium of one hundred dollars an hour. I'll invoice you every week."

"Done," Otto responded.

"What help are you looking for? Are we still taking about a search for the brooch or something else?"

"As I said the other day, the brooch is valuable, and the Society wants to make sure it's recovered."

"I see. And why did you leave me a fake blackmail note at the crime scene?"

"What do you mean?" Otto said, startled. "I certainly did not."

"Yes, you did. I found a letter addressed to you that demanded cash in return for silence about unspecified acts, a letter that miraculously survived the fire. Even if it were genuine, and it somehow had passed through the flames — perhaps by soaking up just enough water from a fire hose to avoid incineration — a careful search must have been conducted by the arson investigators. It would have been seen. You put it there several days after the blaze, assuming I would do my own investigation."

"All right," Otto conceded. "I suppose I owe you an explanation."

"I'd say so. In fact, I'd say the number of explanations you owe me is rising."

They turned off the highway into Chicago's suburbs. This farmland that once surrounded the city is now mostly shopping centers. These are nestled between treeless housing tracts with cul-de-sacs and bucolic names referencing displaced Indian tribes or eighteenth-century English aristocracy or the creeks and rivers that fed the farmland that was subsumed to build the homes.

They turned onto a road leading to an oasis of acreage that appeared to be a horse farm, an assumption confirmed by a sign that read "Paradise Equine Center." Mandrake parked the car beside a barn.

"Is Beatrice a horse?" Cummings deduced.

"Of course," Otto said, getting out of the car. He began to strip off his clothes. Mandrake took several wooden hangers from the trunk and neatly hung them.

"I run with her three times a week," Otto explained. "It's how I stay in shape."

Once naked, Otto scurried over a low metal fence and into a meadow. A brown mare with lustrous locks and a dappled coat snorted in his direction and turned and trotted away. Otto chased after her.

Mandrake first hung the hangers neatly from a hook in the car's rear interior, and then he removed a flask of coffee from a picnic hamper nestled on the floor on the front passenger side. He poured a cup for Cummings.

"Wad ye be awantin rugelach dos morgn?" Mandrake asked.

Since Cummings had no idea what Mandrake was saying, he smiled blankly in response.

About a half hour later, Otto returned to the car, breathless and sweating. Mandrake picked up a nearby hose, thoroughly drenched Otto and then handed him a plush bath towel. Otto dried himself and dressed.

As Mandrake sped them to their next destination, Cummings attempted to resume the conversation.

"You were going to explain the note you left for me," Cummings began.

"Please," Otto said, "give me a few moments to catch my breath."

Cummings observed they were headed from the western suburbs to the northern ones. There, they pulled in front of a chocolatier. Mandrake went in and returned with what Cummings gleaned from the conversation was several pounds of an obscure Belgian chocolate.

They headed west and north, driving into a less populous area. Mandrake turned into a long driveway marked by a sign that read Old MacDonald's Farm. There, Mandrake loaded a case of organic sheep's milk into the trunk.

"I use it to bathe Barbara Cartland," Otto explained to Cummings.

Next they went due north, where they visited four florists in search of two bunches of sufficiently fresh calceolaria.

Finally they headed south to the Magen David Pet Cemetery, where Mandrake distributed yarmulkes to Otto and Cummings.

"It's the anniversary of Charlotte Bronte's death," Otto explained as they walked through the main gate. "She was a Canaan dog from an Israeli breeder."

They came to a small mausoleum at which Otto recited the Kaddish from a transliterated printout while Mandrake donned a prayer shawl and davenned, swaying and chanting with great enthusiasm in what Cummings assumed was Scotchified Hebrew.

Cummings had had enough.

"If you want me to work with you on this matter, you must answer my questions," Cummings said at the conclusion of the prayers. "Why did you leave that letter at the crime scene?"

"I'm being blackmailed," Otto explained. "I thought you'd be more likely to believe me if you discovered this for yourself."

"Why wouldn't I believe you?"

"Because, though I've never understood why, people rarely seem to take me seriously."

"Did you make up that story about the Craddock Brooch? I mean, that the Society wants it back?"

"It is valuable, and it is missing. The brooch wasn't on Surendra's body when she was removed from the building. I looked for it in the rubble. Mandrake did, too. It wasn't there. You see, I think the brooch may have something to do with my circumstances."

"And what circumstances are those?"

Otto reached into his coat and pulled out two ornately calligraphed envelopes. He handed them to Cummings. Inside, Cummings found handwritten note cards of the finest manufacture, edged with black in the manner of Victorian mourning stationery.

The first note read: *Need we remind you of the consequences if the truth becomes known? We demand $25,000 now and subsequent payments to be announced later. We will be in touch with instructions.*

The second note read: *This is not a friendly game of chess. You must comply or there will be consequences. We will be in contact soon.*

"When did you receive these?"

"During the last ten days. They were slipped under my door. Nothing else has occurred. I haven't been contacted by anyone."

"Do you have any idea who these might be from? Why would someone wish to blackmail you? And what information would they blackmail you with?"

"I cannot imagine."

Cummings didn't believe him but pressed on. "They have a rather historical look about them. Do you suspect someone in the Mathers Society?"

"No one I can think of."

"Do you have any particular friends in the Society — or particular enemies?"

"I don't have any enemies, but I do have one friend, Tom Daniels. We met in college. Most of the other students thought I was terribly odd, but Tom was always kind and loyal. That means a lot to me. Other than Tom, I don't see anyone in the Society outside of meetings. I haven't socialized with any of them, not in the twenty years I've been a member. My schedule is so hectic, I rarely even see Tom."

"What do you know about the victim?"

"I barely knew her. She was Rutley Paik's ex-wife. He's one of the members. She and Crandall Hobbs had some kind of altercation a few months ago. I don't know about what. I saw them arguing after a meeting."

"When?"

"I don't remember. During the winter perhaps?"

"Why did you come to me with these letters rather than the police?"

"I can't go to the police."

"Why not?"

"I just can't."

"You're being evasive."

"It's true. I am. A bit. But I promise I'll tell you the rest soon. Very soon. You must trust me. And you must investigate. I'll pay you one-and-a-half times your usual fee. How's that?"

Cummings knew he was being lied to, and he didn't like it. However, given his present financial circumstances, the offer was difficult to turn down.

"I suppose I could interview the members of the Society."

"Yes! That is just the right way to begin!"

"Very well. I'll speak with the members and see if I can learn anything of interest. Then we'll talk again. You will have to give me a contact list and tell me whatever you know about the various individuals—everything you know about them."

As might have been anticipated, Otto knew hardly anything about anyone, or if he did, he didn't share it with Cummings. However, the contact list was useful. It contained both the Steampunk names by which members were known at Mathers meetings and their actual, usually lackluster, birth names.

Later, Cummings was on the Internet searching for information on Surendra Hickok, whose birth name turned out to be Therese Hickok. He read a few facts he already knew: Therese had co-authored a biography of Evangeline Adams with her sister, whose name was Cosima. Subsequently she had been the sole author of a biography of Wilhelm Reich. The occult publishing house, Trismegistus, published both books.

He also learned some new information.

Therese had been an account manager in a large public relations firm in downtown Chicago. A search of real estate records revealed an address in a modest Western suburb, Forest Park.

Then there was this: Cosima Hickok had been dead for about a decade. A brief obituary in a local newspaper, *The Samaria Journal*, noted that she had died suddenly but did not specify the cause.

As Cummings remembered from his time living in Maine, the village of Samaria was very near Horeb. In fact, it was the next town over.

Nine

Cummings was uncertain about the best strategy for interviewing the members of the Mathers Society. Dropping in unannounced is sometimes an advantage. It throws people off, which can lead to revelations. However, people find it unsettling, which irritates them, and thus they are as likely not to say anything as to reveal what they know. He set the timer on his wristwatch, and when it went off, he decided to make appointments.

For geographic convenience, since they lived nearby, Cummings began his interviews with with Crandall Hobbs and Winky Carmello, and with Rothwell Falconer and Lolita Gobble, all of whom lived in the same apartment building.

Unlike most of the other members, Crandall Hobbs and Winky Carmello were, if not actual birth names, names used at Mathers as well as in their day-to-day lives. The couple lived in the Old Irving Park neighborhood, which was close to Cummings in Jefferson Park. Rothwell Falconer and Lolita Gobble were known outside of Mathers as Mary Collins and Glen Smith.

The building in which the two couples lived was an old and stolid residential structure from the 1920s, built on an unusually large lot for Chicago. The building was bounded in front by an iron fence and gate surrounding an expanse of lawn of perhaps half an acre. This was neatly mowed, but no effort had been made to expand the landscape by so much as a single rose bush. Along the right side of the lawn, a concrete pathway led to the building's front steps, which in turn led up to a large, leaded glass door framed with oak. The entrance was adorned with two concrete griffins, corroded by decades of Chicago winters.

As he reached the door Cummings saw an old-fashioned brass buzzer. He leaned in and depressed it, noticing something in his peripheral vision on the corner of the top step: a small, bloody bird carcass carved with some sort of primitive symbols.

Winky, wearing a tight T-shirt and gym shorts that revealed his musculature to advantage, opened the door. His eyes immediately darted to the avian corpse.

"Oh, my! I'm afraid we have another special delivery."

"Why would someone leave a dead bird at your door?"

Winky shrugged. "Being pagan doesn't necessarily mean you have good manners."

"Does this happen often?" Cummings asked.

"I'm afraid so."

"Who do you think might have done this?"

"It's so hard to say! It's intended to be a curse, but I can't say more than that. There are so many occult people in the neighborhood. Astrologers and Tarot readers, of course. There's a hoodoo group. There's a gay men's brotherhood, the Maze of the Minotaur. Crandall calls them the Maze of the Mindless, but he's just being mean. I know there are several Druids. They always paint themselves blue on Easter, which I don't understand, because everyone just thinks they're giant Easter eggs. There's a Kabbalah study circle and a couple of Viking guys that like to hang from trees in the park because that's how their God Odin received enlightenment. Also, there are two or three Traditional Witchcraft groups. They hold rituals in the park in the middle of the night. You're here to talk about the Mathers Society, aren't you? Crandall's expecting you. I hope you'll excuse me, but I was just on my way to see some clients. I walk dogs for a living."

"That must be pleasant," Cummings suggested.

"Oh, yes," Winky said, smiling, "I find them easy to communicate with."

"Do you mean that literally? Like Doctor Doolittle?" Cummings probed.

"I wish, but it doesn't work like that. Animals don't use words. But you already knew that. So what you do is, you think of an image and then project it mentally to the animal, and if the animal wants to talk to you, it responds by projecting an image back. You've got to pick something the animal understands, something in the animal's world that matters to him. And only some animals like to communicate with people this way. Or maybe are able to do it. I don't really know. I tried to talk to all the animals at the Brookfield Zoo, and only an alligator and an owl responded."

"What did they say?"

"The alligator told me he didn't like his food, and the owl said it was very unhappy in its cage and wanted to be let free. That was really sad! Lately, I've been trying to communicate with insects, but so far I haven't made any progress. I've always liked insects. That's what brought Crandall and me together."

"How so?"

"Crandall is a beekeeper. Did you know that? We met when I was massaging a bee at a farmers market."

"Massaging a bee?"

"Maybe massaging isn't the right word. I don't mean, you know, like Shiatsu. The bee flies into your hand, and you gently stroke it. If you do it very carefully, it goes to its happy bee place. I should go see my clients now. Our apartment is the third door on the left."

"Could you spare a little more time? I have a few more questions."

"You want to talk about Surendra, right? I don't really have anything to tell you. I only go to Mathers because Crandall goes. I'm not magickal. You have to be really smart to be magickal — like Crandall."

"Why do you say that?"

"Magick is hard! Way too hard for me! We live in the apartment with the purple door. Just knock."

Winky let Cummings into the building, and Cummings walked down the hall to an apartment with a door painted a dizzying shade of lavender. He knocked. Crandall, wearing jeans and a T- shirt, answered. Even out of Edwardian clothes, his Eurasian features, gray dreadlocks and goatee gave him a sort of Neo-Rastafarian look. His appearance was more Bob Marley than Merlin. Cummings had no idea what to expect when he entered the apartment, but the decor was conventional in a gay, urban way. The rooms were large and had dark wooden floors and oak moldings. The furniture was mostly from the 1940s, restored with period reproduction fabrics. Except for the presence of a television and computers, the entryway and living room could have appeared in a 1947 women's magazine.

There was a pervasive decorative presence of bees on ceramics, throw pillows, several lithographs, even buzzing among flowers on the drapes.

"I understand you keep bees," Cummings said as Crandall ushered him to the sofa.

"I run an organization called Beehold. We're an urban honey producer. We have hives all over the city on roof tops, in abandoned lots, in small gardens. We hire and train people who are unemployed or homeless to tend to the hives and collect the honey."

"That sounds commendable."

Crandall shrugged. "It represents a logical intersection between the collapse of the economy and the collapse of the natural environment. But you're not here to discuss beekeeping, are you?"

"No. Otto asked me to investigate Surendra Hitchcock's death informally."

"Informal though it may be, Otto might have discussed his plans with the Mathers Board of Trustees."

"He didn't?"

"No, though I consider this a breach of protocol rather than poor judgment. I have no objection to speaking with you."

"I understand the Chicago occult community is rather contentious."

"Are there communities that are not contentious?"

"There's a dead bird on your stoop."

"It's a nuisance, nothing more. Most occultists are more addle-brained than menacing. I think of them as sweet little puppies — the lap dogs of the mysterious, if you like. Or if you prefer a human metaphor, they're wedded to silly ideas. Only a small percentage of us are doing the real work."

"And what is the real work?"

"The search for the deeper synergies. I translate obscure works from obscure languages, looking for implicit and explicit relationships. I do not live on a mountaintop, smiting flying reptiles with my wand. This work requires a honed intellect, not super-human skills. As Marion Zimmer Bradley once said, 'I'm not a medium, I'm a large.' Though truthfully, I do own several wands just to keep up appearances, you understand," he added, with a hint of impishness.

"With all due respect, there are more conventional ways to understand the world. The sciences. Mathematics."

"Those are very important pursuits; but did you know that up to the beginning of the seventeenth century, the great scientists were often also occultists? Brahe, Galileo and Kepler studied astrology, for example. Alchemy is what Isaac Newton did — the rest was a hobby. I think such men had a unified approach in their search for the divine plan. Subsequently, for good and ill, the scientific method triumphed, and today we think with bifurcated minds. Very few of us think holistically, and even fewer have a strong intuitive awareness. Those who don't, which is just about everyone, think the occult is at best a waste of time.

"I like to remind the arrogant rational — that's how I refer to such people — that the trouble in the world does not result from the pursuit of the irrational but from certainty. Would you like a few examples of the influence of certainty? The Khmer Rouge, Stalinists, the English Civil War, *Pamela,* the Inquisition, slavery, the conquest of the Americas, the defenestration of Prague, *Pilgrim's Progress,* holy wars, Wall Street bankers, *Valley of the Dolls,* orthodox American psychoanalysts, twelve-tone music, pesticides, every puerile brush stroke of Jacques Louis-David and any number of ferries whose captains let on too many people and tipped the boats."

"Let's talk about the Mathers Society. Can you tell me anything that might prove useful in understanding Surendra's death?"

"I'm afraid the answer is no. I have not observed anything that suggests her death was more than odd, though I must say also that I'm doubtful about spontaneous human combustion. I haven't studied it in depth, but I'm not aware of any cases in which natural causes have been conclusively ruled out."

"How do you think Surendra caught on fire?"

"I don't know."

"Do you think someone in Mathers might have some reason to kill her?"

"As I said, I've observed nothing suspicious."

"I understand you and Surendra had an argument."

"My argument was with Therese, which is her real name, not her Mathers persona."

"What did you disagree about?"

"Therese was in the public relations business. One of her clients was a hotel chain. Her assistant arranged for them to feature my honey in their Midwestern locations — sell it at the front desk, feature it in the breakfast buffet, that sort of thing. But for no apparent reason, Therese quashed the plan. As you might imagine, I was quite angry."

"How angry were you?"

"Mister Wanamaker, I am not the sort of man who suffers fools gladly, but that doesn't mean that I am inclined to murder them."

"One last thing. Beeswax is highly flammable, isn't it?"

"Yes."

Cummings walked up the stairs to the apartment of Lolita and Rothwell, more commonly known as Mary and Glen. Mary opened their door, which was beige. Her hair, which was pink at the Mathers meeting, had been redyed a shade of turquoise. She was wearing jeans and a black T-shirt screened with an Anime unicorn.

Like Crandall and Winky's flat, this apartment was also large, dark and oaken. It was sparsely furnished. A few pieces of 1950s furniture were placed haphazardly around the living room. In the dining room Cummings could see a long table with five-gallon carboys and, in one corner, a replica suit of armor. The room was also dotted with assorted pieces of lumber, woodworking tools and pieces of scrap metal.

"Do you like to be called Mary or Lolita?" Cummings asked.

"Mary's my everyday name."

"Thanks for seeing me, Mary. I've been asked to investigate Therese's death."

"Are you a detective?"

"Something like that," Cummings replied, "but my inquiry is entirely informal. Will Glen be joining us?"

"He's in the bedroom, doing school work."

"School work?"

"He's finishing his master's degree. I'll get him. Sit down anywhere you like."

Cummings sat on a beat-up Mies van der Rohe knockoff. Mary returned with Glen, also in jeans and wearing an unadorned black T-shirt. He shook Cummings's hand; then he and Mary sat on floor pillows opposite Cummings.

"Let's start with some basics," Cummings began. "How do you happen to be living in the same building as Crandall and Winky?"

"We needed a place, and they told us this apartment was vacant," Mary answered.

"We've been here three years," Glen added.

"Almost four," Mary corrected.

"What do you do, Mary?"

"I'm a tattoo artist. I work at Guns and Leather Tattoo. I also moonlight, doing small stuff like temporary tattoos, just to get my name out there. My long-term plan is to open my own tattoo shop."

"She's going to do the tattoos, and I'm going to run the business," Glen contributed.

"And what do you do, Glen?"

"I'm an accountant. I'm finishing my master's in taxation."

"I would guess there aren't too many accountants in the Mathers Society."

"Being an accountant is not who Glen really is," Mary insisted.

"No way. It's just a means to an end because I'm good with numbers," Glen explained. "I'm really all about medieval history. I'm the Vice President of the Shire of the Mossy Turrets. We reenact medieval battles in dormant corn fields."

"Trebuchets and all that?"

"Yeah, but we only hurl foam rubber rocks at plywood castles. We don't want to get anybody killed."

"Glen's also an entrepreneur," Mary said proudly.

"I have two side businesses," Glen explained. "One is historical torture devices. Mostly the small stuff, thumb screws and like that. But I do larger custom items. Last month I made a rack for a couple in New Jersey. I'm going to have a booth at the Renaissance Faire next summer as a way to build word-of-mouth."

"Does the other business involve brewing?" Cummings suggested.

"How did you know?"

"The carboys," Cummings said, pointing to the dining room. "They're used for fermentation."

"I make mead. It comes in two flavors, Black Death and Pestilence. That's orange and mint," Glen continued. "I just make a little right now. The Illinois laws are designed to keep small businesses out of the liquor industry."

"What can you tell me about Therese?"

"She was a very matter-of-fact sort of person," Glen said.

"Not the kind of person who talked about herself," Mary continued.

"We didn't know her well," Glen added.

"We didn't like her much either," Mary confided. "She lied to us."

"About what?" Cummings asked.

"It's a bit complicated. You see, we're polyamorous," Glen explained.

"What does that mean?"

"We're open to outside loving relationships. We had threesomes with her."

"Only a few times," Mary said. "She told us her husband knew, but he didn't. That's Rutley Paik. I think that's his real name. They're divorced, I think."

"We don't go in for deceit," Glen commented.

"I see," Cummings said. "Mary, could you tell me about the inks you use to do tattoos?"

"That's an odd question," Mary responded, seemingly a bit startled. "I use different inks for different purposes—you know, permanent inks, temporary inks, different colors and what not."

"Don't some tattoo inks contain phosphorous?"

"Some, I guess. Why is that important?"

"It's highly flammable," Cummings explained. "In fact, it's used in matches."

Ten

The next afternoon, Cummings visited Tom Daniels. Tom lived in a modest bungalow in Lincoln Park, one of Chicago's most fashionable neighborhoods. The front yard was in disarray. The grass had not been mowed recently, and there were two chaotic perennial beds in desperate need of weeding.

Tom answered the door, wearing a Victorian dressing gown. He looked pallid.

Tom seated Cummings on a plush Victorian settee and offered him some ice tea. As he went to get it, Cummings looked at an array of objects on a tea table in front of the sofa. Some were small Steampunk-inspired objects, such as a dragon made of gears. There were also polished and unpolished stones of various sizes and types and an assortment of items with obscure signs and sigils that identified them as probable amulets and talismans.

After he set a tumbler of tea in front of Cummings, Tom coughed into the same lace handkerchief he'd used at Mathers. "You must excuse me," he apologized, "I'm just getting over a cold."

"I understand," Cummings responded. "I'm not sure how to address you. There appears to be a mistake on the Mathers contact list. You're listed as Queen Victoria but with two real names, Jules Verne and Tom Daniels."

"Actually my real name is Jules Verne. No one believes me, so I go by Tom Daniels."

"Is that so? Are you a descendant of Jules Verne?"

"He was my great-great-great uncle."

"These are interesting," Cummings said, indicating the objects on the tea table.

"Oh, yes. I've collected them over the years. I started when I was an undergraduate. They help me in all manner of ways."

"Do they? For example, what is this one?" Cummings asked, pointing at random to a sigil-covered object.

"That's a Seal of Jupiter. It brings luck and opportunity."

"And this one?" Cummings said, pointing to another.

"That is a bind rune. It's Norse. Its purpose is to protect against enemies."

"Do you have many enemies?"

"No more than most people."

"Perhaps you can tell me something about the Craddock Brooch."

"The what?"

"The piece of jewelry that Surendra was wearing when she died."

"I don't know anything about it."

A vacuum cleaner started in an adjacent room.

"I must apologize," Tom continued. "My cleaning person, Glenda, is here. She always comes on Tuesdays. Usually I go out while she's working, but I didn't today because of this cold."

"Have you been a member of Mathers long?" Cummings said, speaking over the noise.

"I've been in Mathers for a long time," Tom said, also speaking louder. Cummings observed the veins bulging in Tom's forehead as he did so. He seemed to be exerting himself even to engage in conversation.

"I've known Otto even longer," Tom continued. "We met in college. He's been a great friend. He's helped me with my writing. Most people think I'm a trust fund dilettante, but he's always taken me seriously."

"What do you write?"

"I'm working on a serious historical novel, but I also write Christian erotica for pocket change."

"Is that a literary genre?"

"Yes. There's a formula: torrid sex followed by repentance, baptism and the Rapture. My publisher tells me the demographic is twenty-five- to thirty-five-year-old white, married, born again moms who live in trailer parks."

"What can you tell me about Surendra that might be helpful?"

"Not very much, I'm afraid. I barely knew her. She wasn't very friendly. I always thought she was shy."

"Did you notice that she had any particular conflicts with anyone in the Mathers group?"

"No."

"All right then. Thank you for your time."

"That's all?"

"I believe so," Cummings said, getting up and heading for the door. As he did so, he noticed two white paper bags from a chain drug store lying stapled shut on a side table. He wasn't able to read the labels.

Anunciación Hollingberry lived on Lake Shore Drive, known affectionately by the locals as LSD, where the availability of street parking was scarce, and the cost of garage parking was titanic. Reflecting on his tenuous economic circumstances, Cummings made sure to get a receipt from the garage so he could bill the expense back to Otto.

Anunciación's apartment was gargantuan; one practically needed binoculars to see the far wall from the main entrance. The flat was on a high floor with many windows framing an expansive view of Lake Michigan and was furnished primarily with eighteenth-century American furniture.

"Windsor chairs, aren't they?" Cummings said, pointing to a pair.

"How do you know that?"

"I lived in Maine for a few years."

"They're reproductions, but no one in the Midwest knows the difference, don't you know. Chicagoans appreciate only two types of décor, Arts and Crafts and Mid-Century. Honestly, they can't tell a Queen Anne settee from Marie Antoinette's bed pan."

Aesthetics, and the cultural history and dictates that went along with it, was not an area in which Cummings had any particular passion or knowledge. Still he nodded, not wishing to appear stupid.

"Would you like a sherry?" she continued. "It's Portuguese and very dry, as arid as the great dunes of the Sahara, don't you know."

"When we met at Mathers, you were telling me about your mother," Cummings said after Anunciación had delivered his drink.

"Yes. She was a ballerina with a passion for stalactites."

"Were you raised in Europe?"

"Only for a time. Mother married an American military officer, and we went to live in Manhattan. Mother used to say that if he were a cocktail, he'd be one part gin, two parts money and three parts bastard.

"It was during this time that I discovered Mister Balogh, a lovely Hungarian gentleman who taught astrology classes in Greenwich Village. This infuriated my stepfather. Then dear mama was run over by a taxi outside of Bendel's, and my stepfather sent me to a convent school in the Dakotas. That didn't last long. I was expelled for fortune telling. Shortly thereafter, my stepfather died of apoplexy. I arranged a lovely funeral mass for him. I asked the stone mason to carve a wisp of poison ivy on his headstone. I wanted to be absolutely sure that God would recognize the son-of-a-bitch. Then I moved to Chicago, where a few months later I met my late husband, Alfred, who died when I was only twenty-seven. He was a drunk, but at least he left me a few dollars. Did you ask me a question?"

"About Surendra," Cummings interjected.

"Surendra. Yes. She was a very private person. I barely knew her, but I adored her. It's my sweet nature, don't you know."

"Do you have any idea who might have wanted to kill her?"

"Kill her? You don't think she was murdered?"

"Yes, I do. So do the police."

"But she burst into flames!"

"Spontaneous combustion is unproven. I know it's difficult to imagine someone committing such a horrible murder, but it appears someone did."

A few minutes later Cummings made his excuses and moved on to his next appointment. This was with Mandrake Kinnaird.

"How well did you know Surendra Hickok?"

"I be standin' me ben at the Mathers fuid queue, and she be ahin me and we begin aschmoozing 'bout me Toby jugs."

"I'm sorry. Could you repeat that, please?"

Eventually, through a process similar to the parlor game Charades, Cummings came to understand that: (1) Mandrake had met Surendra in the buffet line at a Mathers meeting, (2) they did not know each other well, (3) they had a brief conversation about Toby jugs, whatever they were, which (4) Mandrake collected. Later Cummings looked up Toby jugs on the Internet and discovered that these were pottery objects, often in the shape of heads, first made in England in the eighteenth century.

"I was never actually a member of the Mathers Society, though I'm sure many of the regulars thought I was," Rutley Paik told Cummings when he visited him. "I attended a lot when I was married to Therese because she wanted to go, although sometimes I couldn't make it because I was working. I'm a fireman. I went to this last meeting only because she invited me."

"But you knew she was a member?"

"Yes."

"Did she speak to you about her Mathers activities?"

"Do you mean while we were married? Some, but she didn't say anything deep—I mean, anything worth repeating now that might explain ..." He paused for a moment, emotion making it difficult to finish the sentence, then continued. "... help explain what happened to her."

"What about after your divorce?"

"We were friendly, but we went our separate ways. We weren't that close when we were married. That's why we ended it."

"I understand she was unfaithful to you."

"I'm not the jealous type. There were real problems. We weren't good for each other."

"In what way?"

"Neither of us was much of a talker. You put two people together who don't know how to say what they need to say, you've got yourself a real problem."

"Can you tell me anything about the Craddock Brooch?"

"What about it?"

"What exactly was it?"

"What do they call it, a reliquary? That's the word. You know, like the remains of saints in churches, only this one was pagan. It was a piece of that Craddock woman's leg bone. It was removed after her death and set into a pendant. Creepy, huh? It was supposed to heal people or something. Total nonsense, if you ask me, but you know how it goes when you're married. Discretion is the better part of keeping your mouth shut, or whatever that saying is."

"Do you know where Therese got the brooch?"

"At an auction, I think."

"When?"

"I don't remember. Sometime in the last five or six years."

"Do you know if she sold the brooch at auction herself and then purchased it back?"

"No way. She loved that thing. Anyway, why would somebody do that?"

"The brooch was sold twice at auction during the last few years. I'm eliminating possibilities. I don't suppose you know who the previous owner was?"

"No idea."

The next afternoon Cummings visited the home of Surendra Hickok in Forest Park. Sequentially, Forest Park is the second suburb heading west from Chicago from Oak Park. Unlike Oak Park, Forest Park is what would have been called middle class in the decades of the twentieth century, when the middle class was still thriving. Its downtown, Madison Street, was still filled with unpretentious shops and taverns, and perpendicular side streets were lined with simple but inviting wood frame homes.

One of these homes was Therese's. It was square and sturdy with decorative wooden shingles and large picture windows. The house was set far back from the street, and the expansive front yard had been turned into a large garden with vegetable, perennial and annual beds.

As Cummings arrived he noticed a middle-aged man in overalls and a weathered straw hat pulling weeds.

"What a lovely garden!" Cummings said, approaching the exterior fence.

"Thank you. It was my sister's," the man responded.

"Therese?"

"You knew her?"

"I met her. Like Therese, I moved here from Maine."

"Did you?" the man said, extending his hand. "Samson Hickok."

"Cummings Flynn Wanamaker," he replied, shaking it.

"Where in Maine are you from?"

"Horeb."

"Really? We're from Samaria."

"I know Samaria well."

"You do know what happened to Therese?"

"Yes. I'm so sorry for your loss."

Samson sadly nodded his head. "I'm just cleaning up the place. We're going to sell the house. How do you know Therese?"

"I didn't know her well. I understand she wrote a book about Wilhelm Reich."

"I didn't read her books. Too oddball for me."

"Did Therese know someone named Chess Biederman by any chance?"

"Why do you ask?" Samson responded, apparently surprised by the question.

"He owned a small factory in Horeb. His body was found recently."

"I'm familiar with the name," Samson replied tentatively.

"I understand your sister Cosima died, too, about ten years ago, if I'm not mistaken. Do you mind if I ask what she died of?"

"Who are you again?" Samson asked.

"Cummings Flynn Wanamaker. I've been asked to investigate Therese's death."

"Why are you investigating?"

"Just informally. For the Mathers Society. That's the organization that ..."

"I know what it is," Samson said with an increasing tone of distrust. "Why did they hire someone to investigate?"

"They want to know what happened."

"I think the police are working on that. Are you working with the police?"

"No. As I said, I was asked to investigate informally by members of the Mathers Society. As you might imagine, they are quite upset about what happened."

"I'm sure they are. So am I. If you'll excuse me, I've got a lot to do," Samson said and turned back to the garden.

Back in his car Cummings considered what he'd learned through his interviews, although he realized there wasn't much — or at least not much that was conclusive. This and plotting his next steps were enough to keep Cummings intellectually engaged as he drove home.

Eleven

As the result of an impromptu visit to a yarn store several years earlier, Odin and Luther had developed a passion for the woolly arts. Luther was drawn to making colorful sweaters, while Odin was fond of making scientific and mathematical artifacts in yarn, such as Mobius strips and human brains. These enthusiasms now led them to embark on a yarn crawl.

A yarn crawl is similar to a pub crawl. Fiber shops in a given locale offer various incentives to encourage knitters to drop by and spend money. There were twenty-seven knitting shops within a one hundred-mile radius of Chicago participating in this year's crawl, and Odin and Luther were determined to visit them all. Rockland and Cummings, noble and patient spouses that they were, had agreed to come along for the ride.

Odin and Cummings's financial circumstances had not improved. There had been a discussion before setting out that Odin was just to look at yarn but not actually to buy any. In spite of this there were already several bags of new projects in the trunk of the car, and they had only just left store nine, Purls and Curls, so named because there was yarn in the front and a beauty salon in the back.

"Odin, please," Cummings implored, "we can't be spending money now."

"Do not berate him, Cummings," Luther said. "At least he does not spend your household money on gin and floozies."

"I am not at all sure," Rockland said, "that the term floozy may be applied in a gender-neutral way."

"Is there not a comparable phrase for wayward boys?" Luther drawled.

"No," Rockland said definitively, "this is one of the many linguistic instances in which girls are sluts, and men are virile."

"I have never understood that," Luther continued. "We don't have these double standards when we talk about other species. For instance, I have never heard the female *Agkistrodon piscivorus* referred to as a slut, even though there is no one I am aware of with warm feelings for *Agkistrodon piscivorus.*"

"Mankind reserves its harshest judgments for amorous women, not poisonous snakes," Rockland said.

Luther nodded.

"In any case," Cummings said, looking at Odin, "don't buy any more yarn."

The conversation lapsed for a few minutes as they drove on toward shop number ten, Sheep Ahoy. Rockland finally broke the silence.

"How is your investigation going?" he asked Cummings.

"I'm informally interviewing the members of the group that were present when the victim died."

"Does informally mean you're proceeding out of personal interest, or that someone is paying you?"

"It means I don't have a detective's license."

"Why don't you get one?"

"I'm ineligible. The only way you can become a licensed private detective in Illinois is if you've previously been in law enforcement, which I haven't."

"That's a shame," Rockland responded. "All of those people reaching out to you."

"What do you mean?" Cummings asked.

"Didn't you say you received a number of phone calls requesting help after the story about you in the newspaper?"

"Yes, but I haven't even listened to the messages."

"Why not?"

"Because I'm not a licensed detective, and there's nothing I can do to help them," Cummings said.

"You may be able to work with some of them discreetly. In any case you might as well find out what they want," Rockland continued. "Who knows? There might be an interesting case."

Some hours later, after taking many bags of wool, which Odin assured Cummings would be paid for out of retirement funds if absolutely necessary, into the house, Cummings reviewed his unplayed phone messages. There were more than he'd remembered, about fifteen in all.

Cummings decided to return all the calls. As Rockland implied, there was always the possibility someone might be willing to hire him informally.

"Hello. This is Cummings Flynn Wanamaker."

"I own a bar. It's got a urinal. In the men's room. It keeps breaking. I keep getting it fixed, and it keeps breaking. I think it's my former business partner. He had a sex change. Could you do a stakeout?"

"I know this is a little unusual, but I think my cat is an incarnation of Thomas Jefferson."

"Mrs. Cafferty? This is Cummings Flynn Wanamaker."

"Speak up! I'm hard of hearing."

"This is the detective in the newspaper. You called me about your husband's death. I understand you think he may have been murdered."

"He was a driving instructor. He worked for the Motor Vehicle Department for thirty-seven years."

"I don't understand."

"He flunked lots of nasty boys on the road test."

"Do you think one of them may have killed him?"

"I just said so."

"I see. Tell me about the circumstances of his death."

"What do you mean? He died."

"Was there evidence he was murdered? Lacerations or bullet wounds, for example?"

"That's what I'm calling you for."

"I've committed seventeen murders, but the police think I made it up. Do you help people with communication problems?"

"This is Cummings Flynn Wanamaker. You contacted me about a missing head?"

"That's right! My father got it at the 1964 Republican Convention. Dad was instrumental in getting his state delegation to switch their votes from Nelson Rockefeller to Barry Goldwater. Senator Goldwater gave it to him as a thank you present."

"And what sort of head was it?"

"A shrunken head. Goldwater said it was Hubert Humphrey, but I think it was actually a World War II relic from South Pacific cannibals. It's definitely a real human head. I know because I had it appraised on one of those television antique shows."

"You say it's missing?"

"Yes. There was a break-in at my home. Nothing else was taken. I called the police and told them that my ex-husband was responsible, but they aren't doing anything."

"Why do think your ex-husband took it?"

"He didn't do it himself. He's in prison. But he put someone else up to it. He knows how much I love that thing!"

"So he took it to upset you?"

"Yes. He was embezzling money from his employer, and I testified against him. That's why he's in prison. I went down there to confront him. He wouldn't see me, but I think he'll see you."

"Why do you say that?"

"Because he'll figure that if I've sent a detective, I'm serious about building a case against him; and if I can build a case, he'll get more prison time. So he'll see you just to deny everything. You tell him that if I get my head back, I won't press charges. He's not a fool. He'll make sure I get it back, and that's all I want!"

"There's no guarantee things will go the way you want."

"It's worth a try, isn't it? Please, Mister Wanamaker. It's just a day's work. I'll pay you a thousand dollars in cash. Won't you please help me?"

The case was silly, though at least plausible compared to the others, and the thousand dollars seemed persuasive.

"I'm not a licensed private detective. I only work informally with clients, you understand."

"I understand. Just go see him."

As Cummings anticipated, the visit did not go as hoped —
with a surprise. The embezzler refused to see him. As he was
leaving the visitors' waiting area, contemplating if he'd have
to return the thousand dollars, he saw someone he didn't
expect: Otto Verissimo. Otto was sitting on a bench, perusing
a magazine.

"I suppose it's obvious that I'm surprised to see you here,"
Cumming said.

"Why is it more surprising that I'm here than you are?"
Otto said calmly. There was nothing in his tone or manner to
suggest that this chance meeting disturbed him or he was
pleased about it either.

"My interests are such that a visit to a prison is not
entirely unexpected," Cummings replied, "whereas the same
cannot be said of you. Or is this research? Perhaps you're
locating your next book in a penitentiary."

"I'm visiting someone."

"May I ask whom?"

"There's no reason you shouldn't know. Edgar Diderot. He
was convicted of burglarizing my former neighbors. Falsely
convicted."

"How do you know that?"

"Because I saw the burglars leave my neighbor's
apartment, and he wasn't one of them."

"Did you tell the police that?"

"Of course I did! But my former partner, Louis, who
wasn't even there when the crime occurred, said he had seen
the burglars too, and he was absolutely sure Edgar was with
them. The jury believed Louis rather than me."

"I don't understand. Why would Louis lie?"

"He was a scoundrel. We were breaking up. He'd stolen a
lot of money from me and had taken up with someone else.
Perhaps he thought he could use it as leverage."

"So you visit Edgar?"

"I do what I can to help. I visit when I can. I assist with his legal bills. That's the whole truth. Please let it go now," Otto said, suddenly overwrought. "Being in this gruesome place is difficult enough."

A guard called Otto's name, and he rose to go into the visiting area.

Later Cummings searched the Internet to see what, if anything, he could learn about Edgar Diderot. He found nothing. Apparently the case was just another common crime in a large city, of insufficient interest to attract newspaper or television coverage. Perhaps the Diderot matter was entirely unrelated to the Mathers case, but it did seem remarkably odd to run into Otto in a prison.

Cummings wasn't sure what to expect when he arrived at Clarkson's for the Fine Jewelry and Couture Auction. He didn't go to auctions. He was surprised to discover, for example, that although the sale seemed to focus primarily on jewelry and clothes, it also contained ceramics, rugs, furniture and other objects. Perhaps, Cummings theorized, this rounded out what would otherwise have been insufficient inventory.

It was also unclear how much, if any, relevance this auction might have to the Mathers case. Whatever their interest in Britten, with the exception of Anunciación and Tom, the Mathers members did not appear to have the means to indulge in financial frivolities. As he passed the weathered lions and walked in the door of the auction house, he considered that there was a strong probability this visit might be a bust.

The crowd assembled at Clarkson's was large and boisterous, a demographic smorgasbord of Chicago humans.

The group was so large and diverse that Cummings wondered if going to auctions was some kind of honored Chicago pastime, like watching baseball or bribing politicians.

While perusing the crowd, Cummings wandered among the racks of clothes and display cases, feigning an inspection of the finery. Within five minutes he saw two people he recognized from the Mathers Society.

"This is a surprise!" Cummings said, approaching Tom Daniels and Winky Carmello, who were standing together, chatting.

"No more than seeing you here," Tom responded pleasantly. "I'm just hanging out with Winky," he volunteered.

"Is your cold better?" Cummings asked, although it didn't appear that Tom was any healthier.

"Yes. Thank you for asking," Tom said.

"I'm here to buy the Britten lingam for Crandall," Winky offered, "if the bidding doesn't go too high. I hope you're not bidding, too."

"No, no. My partner likes old tweed coats. I thought I might surprise him," Cummings lied, trying to remember what a lingam was.

"I saw some old Burberrys over there," Winky said, pointing to a picked-over rack of vintage men's clothes.

"I'll take a look. Good luck," Cummings said, going toward the coats. He pretended to peruse them as he continued to scan the room. In one corner he noticed Rutley Paik. Rutley turned and saw Cummings. Clearly, he wasn't pleased to see him. Cummings waved, then approached him.

"Rutley, I wouldn't have thought auctions were your thing."

"You're right about that," Rutley explained with a forced smile, "but our conversation about auctions the other day got me to thinking it might be fun to go to one. I had the day off, so here I am."

"Are you planning to bid on anything?" Cummings said casually as he considered possible reasons why Rutley might actually be there.

"I haven't decided yet."

"Good luck to you!"

Cummings felt a hand on his shoulder. It was Mary Collins. Her hair that day was a subdued shade of violet, an exact match for her 1950s sweater set.

"Hello there! I didn't know you guys were coming to this. I just saw Tom and Winky."

"Really?" Cummings feigned surprise. "Have you seen anyone else here from Mathers?"

"I don't think so."

"Are you here for the Emma Hardinge Britten items?" Cummings asked.

"I don't know even know who that is. I'm here to bid on some Polynesian tattoo needles."

"What do you plan to do with them?"

"Who knows? Wear them in my hair or through my nose or something. Who was that woman you mentioned? Emma something?"

"I understand she was a prominent nineteenth-century occultist," Cummings explained. Just then he noticed Mandrake Kinnaird peering into a display case a few feet away.

"I've never heard of her," Mary replied, "but there were so many famous occultists back then, you can hardly keep track of them. Have fun! I'm going to grab some champagne."

"Good luck with the needles," Cummings said. "It's nice to see you, Rutley." Rutley nodded in reply as Cummings walked away.

Cummings approached Mandrake.

"Hou's aw wi ye?" Mandrake said, smiling. "Otto is up to high dow, nearly to bowking. His naig Beatrice is peely-wally, that be the blether from the bern yaird. So Otto he go daunder over, and I come to the auction hoose like a *schlemiel* to be getting me Toby jugs. But I say, sic as ye gie, sic wull ye get."

Cummings nodded, noting that he was beginning to understand some of what Mandrake said to him, which seemed to be progress.

For the next half hour Cummings feigned interest in the merchandise as he observed the Mathers members he'd already identified and scanned the crowd to see if others appeared.

No additional Mathers members turned up, or at least Cummings didn't see any. The members who were there looked at auction items and sipped champagne. Tom took Mandrake aside for a moment and handed him a hardcover book. Squinting, Cummings could just make out the cover. It was one of Otto's books, *Love's Tender Chainmail*.

An announcement was made that the auction was about to begin. Cummings positioned himself in the back of the gallery on a raised seating platform, allowing for a comprehensive view of the assembled buyers. The Mathers members were spread throughout the room. Tom and Winky sat together, but Rutley, Mandrake and Mary sat alone. This seemed odd to Cummings. Even if they didn't know each other particularly well outside of their meetings, wouldn't they be likely to congregate?

The auction proceeded, as auctions do, in a frenzy of rising and falling paddles. Cummings took a small pad from his pocket and noted the item numbers and successful bidders of the Britten lots. However, the sale proceeded at such speed that he wasn't entirely sure he'd accurately recorded the information.

Winky bid on the Britten lingam but was quickly outbid. He did not bid on anything else.

Mandrake's experience was similar; he bid only on a lot of three Toby jugs but quickly dropped out.

Mary was successful in her quest to acquire the Polynesian tattoo needles — hardly a startling outcome, as she was the only person who bid.

Tom and Rutley didn't bid on anything.

After the auction ended Cummings did his best to discreetly follow the five Mathers members as they left the building, but he was only partially successful. He saw Winky and Tom walk out of the building together. They seemed to be walking toward the parking lot. He observed Mandrake leave the auction with the book Tom had given him.

He glimpsed Mary going around to the side of the building to its loading dock, presumably to pay for and retrieve the needles she had purchased. As she did so, she passed Rutley. She stopped and reached for him, then leaned over to kiss him.

"Not here," Rutley said, pushing her away and walking in the direction of his car.

While this was unexpected, Cummings wasn't sure what its exact significance might be. Hoping that the auction staff might have dispersed to help customers with their purchases, Cummings went back into the main reception area to snoop.

On the reception desk he discovered a list. It contained client numbers, a check box indicating buyer or seller, and lot numbers. Sales prices had been written in by hand.

He checked his list against this one.

He looked for the two bidder numbers, CB234 and CB175, that he had previously identified as sellers of the Craddock Brooch.

CB234, likely Therese, based on his conversation with Rutley, did not participate in the day's auction. No surprise there, as she was dead. But CB175 sold an item that had brought eleven thousand five hundred dollars. Cummings could not recall what it was.

He verified the purchase prices of the Britten lots, most of which came from seller CB788.

Unfortunately, the auction house list did not include any identifying information about sellers. He quickly searched the desk, hoping to find a printout of such a list, but was not successful. The approaching footsteps of a returning staff member forced him to step away hurriedly.

When he arrived home, Cummings discovered a post card from Deuteronomy Smelt in the mail. The front included two lobsters wearing bibs and holding forks in their claws. The caption read "Greetings from Maine."

Cummings flipped the card over and read, "I've uncovered new information that I cannot discuss by telephone. When are you coming back to Maine?"

Cummings dialed Deuteronomy's number.

"The Smelt residence," Elektra chirped in her practiced telephone answering manner.

"Hi. This is Cummings Flynn Wanamaker. May I speak to Deuteronomy, please?"

"Hold the wire," she said, putting the receiver down. A few moments later Cummings heard what sounded like pounding followed by muffled conversation.

"Mister Deuty say you comes visit."

"Please ask him if he knows a Cosima or Therese Hickok."

"Hold the wire," she said again. When she returned, the answer was "Mister Deuty not wish to speak of this on phone." Then she disconnected.

Next Cummings phoned Ernestine.

"Do you know a Cosima or Therese Hickok?"

She thought for a moment and said, "I believe I know the family slightly. They are from Samaria, aren't they?"

"Yes. That's them. Two sisters. Therese was killed in Chicago recently. Cosima died some time ago."

"Isn't that wicked awful! Do you think this has something to do with what happened to Chess?"

"I don't know. There's no actual evidence to link them. Still, it seems odd they're from adjacent villages. And then there's the Wilhelm Reich connection. What are the chances of that?"

"That may be, but remember what they say: If you see horse droppings, don't be looking for zebras."

Twelve

Horses or zebras or both? Cummings didn't know, but the moment seemed right to pause and consider what might be trotting by and whether or not it had stripes.

What did he actually know about the crime? Therese Hickok had combusted while giving a lecture, almost certainly not spontaneously. Chess Biederman's remains had been found in a shrink-wrapped boat. Therese lived in Chicago but was from Maine. She worked in public relations and had written several books, including one on Wilhelm Reich. Chess lived in Maine, one village away from Therese's birth place, and manufactured orgone boxes, invented by Wilhelm Reich. Chess wanted to write a book on the Cold War.

And what of the other players in these dramas?

In Therese's case it was a large cast. Otto Verissimo, whose role was unclear, was very odd. To use a favorite word of one of Cummings's former employers, Otto was ineffable. The others — Anunciación, Crandall, Winky, Mary, Glen, Rutley, Tom, and Mandrake — were equally eccentric, though perhaps less obviously withholding information.

All these individuals were present at the meeting at which Therese died and thus had opportunity.

Any of them might have had the means to kill her. Beeswax is highly flammable. So are some tattoo inks. But, of course, any of them might have acquired other flammable compounds.

That left motive. Crandall had been angry with Therese. Mary and Glen were, too. Rutley didn't appear to be upset with Therese, but he had divorced her. Were any of these conflicts significant enough to inspire a gruesome murder?

Finally there were seemingly more minor details. Therese had been buyer CB234. Who was buyer CB175, and was that information relevant?

The circumstances of Chess's murder, beyond the fact that he was dead and not from natural causes, were totally unclear. Chess was popular in Horeb, and no one had any apparent reason to kill him. Not only were there no suspects, there was no obvious reason why there should even be any.

Cummings set his watch timer for thirty minutes and intensely scribbled notes of the various steps he might take to move his investigations forward. The buzzer sounded, and he moved into action.

He phoned Otto. Reaching Mandrake, he requested an appointment with Otto for the following afternoon, a conversation he was reasonably certain had been fully understood by both parties.

He researched Mary, Glen, Crandall, Winky, Rutley, Mandrake and Tom on the Internet. Nothing emerged that contributed substantively to his existing knowledge or contradicted what he knew.

He left his house and walked the half block to Luther's and Rockland's place.

Cummings and Odin had inadvertently introduced Luther and Rockland when they'd invited them to dinner. It was summer. Both arrived punctually, dressed immaculately in linen shirts and slacks. Rockland's arm was in a sling, made of matching linen, due to a recent injury.

That both his guests shared a common interest, prissiness, raised Cummings's hopes for a successful evening. Yet at first the conversation was strained. Luther seemed shy, and Rockland seemed uncharacteristically reserved. Cummings made several thrusts at conversation, but none seemed to penetrate. Then, sometime between the cold carrot soup and the Caesar salad, Cummings mentioned that Luther taught music.

"The organ," Luther added.

"I'm interested in music, particularly Appalachian music," Rockland said, suddenly more animated. "I have a theory: the design of the hammered dulcimer evolved to mimic certain characteristics of indigenous reptiles."

"Isn't that interesting? Do you know the East Tennessee Dulcimer and Autoharp Festival?" Luther asked Rockland.

"I go every year," Rockland said, now truly engaged. "That's where I got this bite," he continued, indicating his bandaged arm.

"I grew up right there, near Friendship," Luther said.

"Where is that?" Cummings asked.

"Oh, let's just say it is somewhere between Arkansas and the Theory of Evolution," Luther replied.

"Then you've been to the festival?" Rockland asked Luther.

"Well, of course," Luther informed him. "I am fond of all kinds of music. Now what is this about reptiles?"

"Are you interested in reptiles?"

"Oh, yes. Death by snakebite is a sort of pastime in my family. For instance, a particularly insistent eastern coral snake killed my grandfather. He was bitten sixteen times."

"Was he?"

"That is the story, although my grandmother and grandfather were known to have their disagreements, and my grandmother could be a very unforgiving woman. So who is to say, in this case, just how accidental *accidental* was?"

"I am currently researching *Heterodon platirhinos,* commonly known as the ..."

"As the eastern hognose snake," Luther said, finishing his sentence. "It eats toads, I believe, though it is not a particular danger to humans."

"That is correct," Rockland said, smiling broadly.

"That puts me in mind of my great-aunt Martha," Luther continued. "She poisoned the toads in her garden after her husband was tragically killed in a fire at the Amphibian House at the Saint Louis Zoo."

"Was she psychotic?"

"No, she was just Southern. Now what is your interest in this particular creature?"

And so it went. From this point on Odin and Cummings ceased to be in the room, at least for Rockland and Luther. By dessert, Rockland and Luther had somehow drifted down the street to Rockland's house, leaving Odin and Cummings alone with their pie and coffee.

Rockland's and Luther's house was, like Odin's and Cumming's home, a World War I era Arts and Crafts bungalow. Cummings climbed the few stairs and banged authoritatively on the heavy brass knocker. Rockland, wearing a silk dressing gown that might have come from a 1930s movie, opened the door.

"I trust nothing dire has occurred."

"Why do you say that?" Cummings asked.

"I say that because it is rare these days that anyone drops in, particularly without calling first. In fact, when someone has something to say, they typically say it on the telephone or text it."

"May I come in?"

"Of course you may come in," Rockland said, moving aside like the Red Sea to create a way forward.

Cummings entered the house. Though he wasn't much on aesthetics, it was difficult for Cummings not to reflect on how different Rockland's house looked now that Luther lived in it. Rockland's restrained taste, all chintz and liquor cabinets, had been dispatched in favor of Luther's darker sensibilities. The living room now looked like the set of a Tennessee Williams play, assuming he'd written one set in a mausoleum. The room was effectively lightless and airless. Although the walls were a pale, ethereal off-white, the windows were covered in heavy, brown velvet drapes. The furniture was somberly upholstered in dark brown and grey prints. Wherever one's eyes rested, one found crucifixes and thuribles and vases of calla lilies and statues of saints and masses of candles.

The air was heavy with lingering incense. Cummings coughed as he sat down. "It's a bit smoky in here," he said.

Rockland rose, pulled back a set of velvet drapes and opened a window.

"Better?"

"Yes, thank you. I'm here for two reasons. One is that I want to ask you a favor."

"Does it involve chemical analysis?" Rockland asked with a certain restrained glee.

"I'm afraid it's more boots-on-the-ground than that. I want to learn more about the various members of the Mathers Society. I wondered if you'd be willing to follow one of them for a few days. His name is Rutley Paik."

"I don't see why not, but why this particular man?"

"He lied to me about his presence at an auction; but more than that, I have an instinct about him."

"An instinct?"

"That's all I can say at this point. I'll email you his address and my notes about him. He's the ex-husband of the deceased. He may be romantically involved with another Mathers member, who is married to someone else."

"And what of the other members?"

"At least five may be worthy of our attention. My suggestion is that you keep an eye on Rutley, and I'll do what I can with the others. Depending on what I observe and you observe, we can discuss a change of strategy."

"That seems reasonable."

"While I'm here, may I borrow a copy of *Love's Tender Chainmail?*"

"Is that one of Mister Verisimilitude's scribblings? The various volumes are over there."

He pointed to an ornately carved Jacobean-style bookcase. There Cummings found the collected works of Otto Verissimo neatly shelved in alphabetical order.

"Would you like some tea? I was just going to brew a pot," Rockland said, rising and walking toward the kitchen.

"Thanks," Cummings replied as he opened *Love's Tender Chainmail* and skimmed the first few pages.

It seemed that the novel was set in the twelfth century in a European city near a great forest. It was snowing heavily. The Black Death had moved on, but now lepers were dropping fingers and noses like pine cones. Brian, son of Cuconnacht of the Adoration of the Blessed Virgin, out of sorts from starvation, was begging by the city gates after losing his position as squire to a noble Lord, Eoghan, son of Aengus Who Rejoices in Divine Providence. Eoghan and Mochan, another knight, had been in love with Brian. When Brian gave himself to Mochan, Mochan betrayed Brian over an as yet unexplained sacramental mystery involving Hildegard of Bingen, Thomas Becket and a donkey with stigmata. Further, it seemed that Mochan had disappeared — no one knew why or where - and Eoghan, who also wasn't feeling well, was rumored to be coming down with the Great Pox.

Rockland returned with a pot of tea and a plate of cookies.

"I'll return the book soon," Cummings said.

"Take all the time you need," Rockland replied.

Early the next morning, after his usual struggle to select what tea to have with what breakfast, Cummings set out to see what, if anything, could be learned by following the various Mathers members.

He passed by Anunciación's apartment building on Lake Shore Drive. There was no activity in front of the building. Counting the floors, he determined where Anunciación's windows were and peered up to them. However, they were too high for this to be much use.

He continued to Mandrake's apartment in Rogers Park, located in the far northeast of the city. Rogers Park, like many Chicago neighborhoods, contained an odd mix of inhabitants. On one side it was primarily Orthodox Jews. On the other it was primarily East Indians. Both had their respective shopping districts on opposite ends of the same boulevard.

As one might guess, Mandrake lived in the Jewish section. As he maneuvered through narrow side streets, Cummings mapped Mandrake's address on his phone. The building was a "two-flat," a common Chicago apartment configuration in which there is one unit on the ground floor and one upstairs.

As Cummings arrived, Mandrake was walking out of the building. Cummings followed him in his car as Mandrake turned the corner onto a main thoroughfare. He headed into a coffee purveyor, Grounds for Rejoicing. Based on the window signs, which were in Hebrew, Cummings concluded the shop catered to the locals.

Cummings parallel parked and waited a few minutes for Mandrake to reappear. When he did, it was with a large cup of coffee in a paper cup and a bagel with a *shmear*. Mandrake scarfed these down as he continued to walk, arriving a few blocks later at a Red Line L-station, as Chicagoans referred to their elevated transit system. Looking at a system map on his smart phone, Cummings saw that this train would take Mandrake to the South Side, presumably to his job at Otto's.

Cummings considered trying to follow Mandrake further, but realized it would be logistically difficult and likely would result in little additive information.

He headed to the Old Irving Park apartment building where Winky, Crandall, Mary and Glen lived.

The rush hour traffic was starting to build by this time, and it took him more than half an hour to reach the building. He arrived around eight-fifteen and managed to find a parking space about a half block away on the other side of the street. This afforded him a clear view of the front door, as well as some protection from being observed.

After a few minutes, during which Cummings scanned FM radio channels, thinking he might be settling in for a long wait, Crandall emerged from the building with a thorny black walking stick. He reached down and picked something up with it. As he lifted it, Cummings saw that it was a dead pigeon. It seemed to be covered in some kind of white substance, as well as blood.

Crandall concentrated intently on it for a few moments as if inflicting a curse. Then he put the bird somewhere on the side of the house; Cummings couldn't see where. This done, Crandall went back into the building.

Cummings continued to fiddle with the radio. Soon Crandall re-emerged with Mary. They seemed to be chatting pleasantly as they walked together down the street. Cummings saw them go into an L-station two blocks away.

More time passed. Winky emerged. He was also headed toward the L.

Seconds later Glen, wearing a suit and tie and carrying a briefcase, descended the front steps. He, too, walked toward transportation.

Cummings waited a quarter of an hour. None of his persons of interest returned. Cummings started the car.

He circled the area until he found a diner. He went in and had a donut and tea. The donut was stale, but the stop served its purpose. It passed some time.

Eyeing the flow-through bag in his mug with contempt, he finished the last of the amber liquid, then turned his attention to some notes he'd made the previous evening. Then he went back to the car and headed for his destination.

This was Beehold, which was located in a low-rise office building in the South Loop on a block with new galleries, cafes and condo buildings.

The office and its decor were crisp but low-budget: clean lines and high-tech laminates. A painted plaster bee hive, which Cummings estimated was four feet high, stood by the reception desk. A young woman sat behind it. She looked up and studied him as he entered.

"Are you here to fix the photocopier?" she asked.

"No," Cummings said, "I'm an acquaintance of Crandall Hobbs. Is he here?"

"He hasn't arrived yet."

"Are you expecting him?"

"Yes."

"May I wait in his office?"

"No, but you may wait there." She pointed to a nearby arrangement of chairs, orchestrated around a low circular table painted with buzzing bees. Cummings sat and perused Beehold's annual report. As is typically the case in such documents, the report was stuffed with pictures of smiling faces. Cummings found this a surprise, as he always did. Given that nonprofits typically seek to resolve horrible and intractable problems, why is everyone always smiling?

Crandall arrived, and Cummings rose to greet him.

"Crandall, Cummings Flynn Wanamaker. We met recently when I ..."

"I know who you are," Crandall said with a quizzical, if pleasant, tone. He seemed surprised to see him.

"I wonder if I might speak with you for a moment?" Cummings asked. "Perhaps in your office?"

"Certainly," Crandall replied, ushering Cummings down a hallway.

Crandall unlocked his office door, and they went in.

Cummings perused the office, looking for any information that might be illuminating. The room was very different from Crandall's apartment. There was no evidence of his pagan life, just a desk with a computer, several chairs and a bookcase full of management texts. Neatly stacked papers covered other surfaces. The only visual adornments were a poster from the Chicago Art Institute of an eighteenth-century English landscape painting of beekeepers and a framed picture of Winky.

"Are you scanning my office for something in particular?" Crandall asked, aware that Cummings was eyeballing his domain.

"I was just admiring your office."

"I like to keep it purely functional. So what can I do for you?" Crandall asked.

"I'd like to buy some honey."

"You stopped by to buy honey?"

"I was in the neighborhood," Cummings lied.

Crandall nodded. "All right. We have some at the front desk."

His next stop was in Bucktown, one of several Chicago neighborhoods in which affluent and stylish young worker bees like to swarm and buy their first overpriced hives. It was also the home of Guns and Leather Tattoos.

Guns and Leather Tattoos was black and bright: black walls, black floors, black ceilings and fluorescent lights. The walls were covered with illustrations of tattoos of every size, color way and theme. There was a reception area in the front with a number of beat-up chairs. Beyond it there was a large room where the work was actually conducted. A capacious industrial cabinet stood on one side of it. Its doors were open, allowing Cummings to see that it contained tubes and jars and bottles of various murky substances, as well as equipment. Cummings assumed there were tattoo inks and the assemblages required to do the actual tattooing.

Mary was working when Cummings arrived, adorning a mass of flesh spread on a table before her. Cummings moved through the reception area to its farthest point and saw that Mary was putting a life-size monarch butterfly on the ample left butt cheek of a young lady.

A facially tattooed, skeletally thin man with grayish skin appeared and stood in front of Cummings, preventing him from going into the work room.

"May I help you?"

"Yes. Do you offer gift certificates? I was going to buy my husband a tweed coat for his birthday, but that didn't work out. So I thought I might get him a tattoo."

"We sure do. What amount were you thinking of?"

They discussed the costs of various tattoos and what scale of gift certificate might be suitable relative to what Odin might wish to have permanently inked. Meanwhile, Mary, a model of professional concentration, never looked up.

Cummings went back to his car. He considered visiting Glen and Winky at work but quickly eliminated that option. His effort that morning had been fruitless, and a glance at a corporate cubicle or the city streets, respectively, seemed unlikely to change that.

Only one possibility remained. Cummings drove to Lincoln Park, where he managed to find a parking space within sight of Tom's bungalow. He took a pair of binoculars out of his glove compartment and waited. Then he waited some more.

Late in the morning Cummings observed Mandrake climb Tom's steps and knock on the door. He carried a copy of *Love's Tender Chainmail*.

In the afternoon, at the agreed-upon time, Cummings rang Otto's doorbell. He was admitted by Mandrake. Cummings passed under the heads of Sebastian's staring African acquaintances and was led by Mandrake to the Parlor of the Orchids. Mandrake seated him and left to get refreshments.

"Good afternoon," Otto said, entering the room with Barbara Cartland trotting behind him, just ahead of Mandrake's return with the tea trolley. Mandrake began to serve tea.

"Did you enjoy the auction, Mandrake?" Cummings asked.

"Auction?" Otto asked.

"Yes," Cummings continued, "Mandrake and I ran into each other at Clarkson's auction house."

"Really? You didn't mention that, Mandrake," Otto responded.

"Aye, aye. Ah went wi' Tom. Tobys wur fur tout."

"Yes," Cummings said, realizing his capacity to understand Mandrake seemed to be increasing still further. "I thought it odd that a few Toby mugs were included in a jewelry and couture auction, but I suppose the more honey you slather, the more flies you attract. I was surprised by your apparent lack of enthusiasm, Mandrake."

"Whit dae ye mean?"

"You dropped out of the bidding very quickly, I thought."

"Aye, it's a said fecht. Them Tobys be a'place in me hame. Genug iz genug."

"Is that the only reason you went to the auction?"

Suddenly Mandrake exploded. "Dinna think ye ken when ye dinna ken, ye schmuck!" Incensed, he marched out of the room.

Otto glanced at Cummings woefully.

"I must apologize," he said. "Sometimes Mandrake gets overly sensitive about his Tobys. They're the closest thing he has to human relationships. If you'll excuse me for a moment." Otto left the room, presumably to soothe Mandrake.

Cummings, seizing the opportunity, moved quickly to the bookcases containing Otto's literary output and scanned the shelves until he located the various hardcover, paperback and foreign editions of *Love's Tender Chainmail*. He pulled from the shelf the edition that seemed to most closely match the one he'd seen Mandrake carrying. This was the English (U.K.)

hardcover, which had a different cover than the American version. He opened it. The pages were glued together, and the interior was hollowed out.

He heard footsteps and hurriedly reshelved the book, but Otto was in the room as he completed the task.

"I was just admiring your work," Cummings explained. "Now that I've met you, I've become interested in your books. I'm reading them. I think this is my favorite so far."

"Which one is that?" Otto asked, pleased that he had acquired a new fan.

"*Love's Tender Chainmail.*"

"Oh, yes. One of my most poignant, I think. I'll be pleased to give you an autographed copy before you leave. I must apologize for Mandrake again. He's having a time out in the kitchen. Do have some rugelach. Now what was it you wanted to see me about?"

Cummings had found more than he was hoping for, but as a way of explaining his presence, he updated Otto in a very limited manner on the status of his investigations.

Cummings was sitting in his car, holding his autographed copy of *Love's Tender Chainmail* and considering whether the day's surveillance was at a logical ending point, when his cell phone rang.

"Cummings, this is Rockland."

"Rockland, where are you?"

"Lincoln Park. I've been following Rutley Paik. He is currently parked on the 900 block of West Dickens Avenue. He's been there for an hour. Can you think what he might be doing?"

"Is he near this address?" Cummings said, consulting his notes and giving a street number to Rockland.

"Yes, right near it."

"That's where Tom Daniels lives."

"Who is Tom Daniels?"

"Another Mathers member."

"Fascinating! Now assuming our Mister Paik is watching our Mister Daniels the way we're watching him, what does that suggest?"

"I'm not sure. Perhaps Rutley knows something about Tom that we don't."

"At the very least," Rockland concurred. "Do you think our Mister Paik has a professional reason to be watching our Mister Daniels?"

"I don't know what that would be. Rutley is a fireman. Can you sit tight for a while and see what happens?"

"I certainly can," Rockland replied. "I'll telephone if there are any developments."

Twenty minutes later, as Cummings sat in traffic on his way home, Rockland phoned again.

"A young woman appeared on foot and got into the car with Rutley. They're heading northwest. I don't know where they're going, but I'm pursuing."

"What does the woman look like?"

"Tall and thin, a little Dutch boy hair cut dyed red."

"That sounds like Mary Collins. She's also a Mathers member and is married to another member named Glen."

"Is she? I'll phone you when they arrive at their destination."

Their destination, as Cummings found out in a subsequent phone call from Rockland, turned out to be a cheap motel in the city's northwest corridor. Rockland watched them park, check in and go to a room.

"This confirms that they're having an affair," Cummings said to Rockland. "I saw them kissing at the auction."

"That seems clear," Rockland agreed.

"It's odd that they chose to meet on Tom's block," Cummings remarked. "Perhaps it's just a coincidence, although neither of them lives nor works near Tom's house, so why meet there?"

"There must be a reason," Rockland theorized.

"Yes. But what is it?"

Thirteen

The next afternoon, Cummings received a call from Ernestine.

"I just heard from a little birdie the results of Chess's autopsy."

"What little bird?"

"Someone who knows someone in the Sagadahoc County Sheriff's office. I did not understand the scientific details, but I do think I understand the thrust of the thing."

"And what is that?"

"It's complicated, you understand. The body was there for months. They don't think it froze until some days after it was put in the boat, so Chess decayed quite a bit at the beginning. The placement of the boat on my land seems to have resulted in much heat from the sun on the front cabin. Although Chess did freeze sooner or later, he also partially thawed a few times. Then there were the animals gnawing at him. So all and all, it seems there wasn't a whole lot of Chess in the state when he was found that it was in when he was lost. They found some of this chemical, and they found some of that chemical, but not enough to be absolutely sure about anything. But there was a fracture on the back of his skull, so he must have been hit wicked good."

"Is that what killed him?"

"I don't think that's clear. Incidentally, I saw Elektra at the store. She asked me to ask you, when will you be visiting Maine again? It seems Deuty is wicked eager to see you."

"Thanks, Ernestine."

The following morning Cummings returned to Rutley Paik's modest bungalow but did not find him home. He left a note, asking him to call Cummings. Cummings was sure he would. Those who are hiding something, as Rutley surely was, are always eager to demonstrate they aren't.

The call came within three hours.

"You left a note at my house?" Rutley asked.

"Indeed I did," Cummings replied. "Thanks for getting in touch. I have just a few more questions, if you don't mind."

"Why would I mind?" Rutley said.

"I'm confused about the Craddock Brooch. You said Therese bought it at an auction."

"Actually, it was a gift from me. She bought it, but I paid for it."

"You bought it? Why did you lie about that?"

"I didn't. I answered the question you asked."

"Why were you at the Clarkson's auction?"

"I told you. I was curious."

"I think you were there because you've been keeping an eye on Tom Daniels."

"Why do you say that?"

"Because my colleague saw you parked in front of his house."

"I was meeting someone. It was a convenient location."

"Neither you nor Mary lives or works in Tom's neighborhood."

"You know about Mary?"

"Yes. Now would you tell me why you've been investigating Tom?"

"Why have you been following me?"

"Why have you been following Tom?"

"I don't have to tell you anything."

"No, you don't. However, you do understand that I'm trying to find out what happened to Therese?"

"Yes, but I don't know why."

"I conduct investigations for the joy of it. I like to figure things out. What about you?"

"I'm a fireman," he said, softening. "That means, among other things, that I know what can happen in an official investigation in this city. I don't trust the experts not to screw things up."

"So your interest is making sure that Therese's murder is solved, just the same as mine."

"I guess so."

"Then let's share information. Honestly, Rutley, my investigation isn't going as easily as I'd hoped," Cummings said.

"I'd say you're doing all right. You figured out about me and Mary," Rutley said with a hint of respect.

"That's true, but that's hardly substantial progress. In truth, I'm working on two murders right now, Therese's and another in Maine."

"Therese was from Maine."

"Indeed she was, and this other murder occurred one village over from hers."

"Where? Do you mean in Horeb?"

"Exactly. So you've been there?"

"Yes. With Therese."

"I don't suppose you recall meeting a man named Chess Biederman?"

"Damn, you don't miss a thing, do you? Therese used to see him once in a while when we were in Maine. I never went along. Like I said, I'm not the jealous type, and I thought it would be a little weird to accompany your wife to visit her ex-husband."

"Therese and Chess were married?"

"I thought you'd sleuthed that out."

"No. I scanned public records, but it didn't turn up."

"That's just the kind of thing that happens in official investigations. Errors occur. Things get overlooked. You see why I'm trying to figure this out myself? Chess and Therese were married only a few months. They were high school sweethearts, and Therese got pregnant. They got married, and then she had a miscarriage. They didn't really want to be married so young, so they got it annulled. They stayed friends. Not close friends, but friends. Therese might hear from him once or twice a year. If we were in Maine, she might meet him for coffee."

"Chess is the other murder victim."

"You're kidding! How can that be? Therese was killed by someone in the Mathers Society."

"How do you know that?"

"It's the only reasonable explanation, isn't it?"

"I don't know," Cummings replied. "Coincidences occur, even improbable ones. Now tell me why you suspect Tom Daniels of murdering Therese."

"The truth? He creeps me out."

"So you've been following him on a hunch?"

"Let's say I've been keeping an eye on him."

"What about the other Mathers members?"

"I've been keeping an eye on them, too, but none of them creeps me out the way Tom does."

"What about Mary?"

"What do you mean? She didn't kill Therese."

"Is she helping you investigate the others?"

"No. She doesn't know what I'm doing."

"But you're having an affair?"

"We're trying to keep it quiet. It's just sex. She keeps saying she's going to tell Glen about it. They have an arrangement."

"But she hasn't told him?"

"Not as far as I know. Believe me, I didn't expect us to get together. Mary had the hots for me and asked me to coffee. I only went to find out what she knew. She didn't know anything, but one thing led to another."

"What about Crandall and Winky and the others?"

"I haven't slept with them."

"I wasn't asking that. What I meant was, do you suspect them?"

"Not so far, but it's not because I've ruled them out, it's because I haven't had much of a chance to watch them. All I'm fairly certain of is that Mary and Glen had nothing to do with Therese's death."

"Why do you say that?"

"Because I've spent a lot of time with Mary and Glen, and they've never said or done anything that raised my suspicions."

"You've spent time with Glen?"

"They like threesomes."

"But you say he doesn't know about you and Mary?"

"He doesn't know about Mary and me as a twosome. It's murky."

"Apparently."

After considering this new information for a time, Cummings decided that as it was a nice day, he might move his cogitation to a nearby park. It was there, while staring absently at bees working a flower bed, that something occurred to him. He pulled out his cell phone.

"Crandall, it's Cummings Wanamaker."

"Indeed. Enjoying your honey?"

"I'd like to talk to you in more detail about your argument with Therese. You said Therese's firm had arranged to sell your honey through one of her clients — a hotel chain, I believe — but she decided abruptly not to proceed."

"That is correct."

"When she did find out what your organization did?"

"I don't know. We didn't talk much about my professional life at Mathers. I told her I ran an eco-friendly social entrepreneurial nonprofit, something like that, and suggested we discuss the possibility of a marketing arrangement with some of her clients. At that point she told me to talk to her assistant. She may not have known the details until things had progressed. Why do you ask?"

"A hunch. Thank you."

Next Cummings phoned Rockland.

"We were correct. Rutley Paik has been trailing Tom Daniels."

"What about the girl?"

"An affair, nothing more. Did I tell you about the murder in Maine?"

"What murder in Maine?"

"I've also been working on a case there. It appears that Therese was married to the victim. I just learned this from Rutley."

"Did you indeed?"

"That being so, I think it's time for a visit. I seem to be at an impasse in Chicago anyway."

"Can you afford it?"

"Not really, but I'll make it cheap. I'll drive. I have people I can stay with. I don't think Rutley has anything to do with the crime. I think it's time to change our focus. Could you keep an eye on Tom Daniels?"

"Why?"

"There's something odd going on there, something that seems to involve that book I borrowed, *Love's Tender Chainmail*." Cummings explained about the hollowed out book.

"It would be my pleasure."

When Cummings told Odin he was going to Maine, he stressed that it would be a quick and inexpensive trip and that he would stay with Ernestine. Odin wasn't as resistant as Cummings had feared.

"I have a job interview on Monday," Odin announced. "I don't know too much about the job, but maybe I'll get it, and it will pay enough that we can stop worrying about money."

"That would be terrific," Cummings agreed. "What company is the interview with?"

Odin suddenly seemed reticent. "I'd rather not say," he replied. "I don't want to jinx it."

Cummings rose very early, loaded up his car and pulled out of his driveway shortly after 6:00 a.m.

In transit Cummings made a few phone calls. One was to Ernestine to tell her he would be arriving that night. He apologized for the late notice, but she didn't seem to mind.

Another call was to his father.

"Dad? It's Cummings."

"Hello, son. I am seeking a ten-letter word that begins with *c* and ends with *y*. The clue is 'not the pen ultimate.'"

"Cacography," Cummings said after thinking for a minute. "It means bad handwriting or spelling."

"You're the best, son," George said. "Here's another puzzle. It's called chilly phrases. The first clue is 'rarely fought.'"

"Cold war," Cummings responded.

"Out damned spot."

"Cold cream."

"Yet still fraught."

"Cold comfort."

"Only plot."

"Cold feet."

"No forethought."

"Cold turkey. Dad, I have to go. I'm on my way to Maine now. I'll call you in the next day or two."

Fourteen

At around 11:00 p.m. Cummings arrived at Ernestine's. He brought in his luggage, flopped exhausted onto the top of a bed in one of the guest rooms and slept until 8:00 a.m.

He took a shower and then placed a call to Deuteronomy. His call was answered by what sounded like an old-fashioned machine with a taped message. The voice was Elektra's, probably reading from a script, as it was the only time Cummings had heard her use English in its unmangled form. He left a message after the beep.

"Hello. This is Cummings Flynn Wanamaker. I'm in Maine for the next few days. I'm staying with Ernestine. I hope to visit you when it's convenient." He left his cell phone number.

Cummings went downstairs and found Ernestine in the kitchen with her housekeeper, Rebecca. He also found a pot of tea and a basket of fresh muffins.

"Elektra phoned last night to ask for your phone number," Ernestine told him. "I told her to tell Deuty you were here. I hope that's all right."

"I just phoned him," Cummings said.

"You know, they dropped the charges against him," Ernestine said.

"He mentioned something about a run-in with the law, but he said it wasn't serious. It didn't seem appropriate to pry."

"He got caught poking around a building in Zion he shouldn't have been poking around, and he was arrested for trespassing. Well, the district attorney is dropping the charges. So that's that."

"I'm sure Deuteronomy is relieved," Cummings said, sitting down and reaching for a muffin.

"I imagine so, but if you ask me, the incident was nothing marrying nothing. An old man out in the evening, more or less minding his own business, shouldn't find himself under arrest."

Cummings found Samson Hickok's address online and got into his car. Samaria, the next village north on Route 240, had a history similar to Horeb's, though Samaria had always been larger and more prosperous. Samaria was founded in the eighteenth century, achieved its economic peak in the nineteenth and declined in the twentieth until, like Horeb, it resurged as a bedroom community.

Two fires around the turn of the twentieth century had destroyed Horeb's waterfront on the Carlisle River. Samaria's downtown remained intact, as did its Greek Revival houses, a legacy of its affluence in the period before the Civil War. Samaria had shops, restaurants and galleries, albeit not very many, and none particularly distinguished.

Cummings located Samson's house and parked on a side street. Their last encounter had not gone well; Cummings knew he'd have to do better this time.

Cummings set the timer on his watch, opened his glove compartment and took out a small pad and pen. He attempted to write down useful, trust-inducing phrases he might casually toss to Samson or whatever member of his family answered the door when Cummings knocked. When the buzzer sounded, he had a half-dozen comments that seemed potentially effective.

He walked toward the house, a late Victorian in need of exterior paint. As in Illinois, Cummings found Samson in the garden. This garden, enclosed by a whitewashed picket fence, was large and regimented—the perennials here, the vegetables there, the herbs at the near end, the fruit trees at the far end— with each section separated neatly by a strip of well-trimmed sod.

Cummings leaned over the fence. "What a lovely day!" he said with perhaps too much enthusiasm.

Samson, who was weeding a vegetable bed, looked up. He studied Cummings for a few moments and then realized who he was.

"I didn't expect to see you again," Samson replied tonelessly.

"I hope you'll forgive me for stopping by. I know I was a bit of an eager beaver when we last met. Sometimes my curiosity gets the better of me."

"What exactly do you want?"

"As you know, I'm looking into Therese's death for the Mathers Society. I'm not working with the police or an insurance company or anyone else. There's nothing tangible for anyone at Mathers to gain here, just closure. Everyone loved Therese."

"And you think I know something useful?"

"I was hoping you might confirm some information. To begin, I'm just curious — did Therese dislike bees?"

"Yes. She hated them. Why do you ask?"

"A guess. What was the cause?"

"She ate some poison honey when she was a child. She was very sick."

"Who poisoned it?"

"No one. It was naturally occurring. The bees made the honey from poisonous plants."

"I see. And what did Cosima die of?"

"A car accident."

"May I ask what happened?"

"What usually happens around here: an icy road during the winter. She lost control and careened into a tree."

"Only one more question. Can you confirm that Therese and Chess were married?"

"Yes, briefly. They remained friends. Therese had an MBA. Chess didn't. Sometimes she gave him business advice."

"This is a really beautiful garden."

"Is there anything else?"

"No. Thank you so much. I appreciate this. Thanks again!"

"Very well then," Samson said, returning to work.

On the way back to the car, while he was congratulating himself on his display of interpersonal sensitivity, something occurred to Cummings. He reached for his cell phone.

"Rockland?"

"Cummings. Aren't you in Maine?"

"I am. I have a toxicology question for you."

"Excellent! I do enjoy toxins before lunch."

"Generally speaking, how prevalent are toxic species among common garden plants?"

"Many common varieties are poisonous in whole or in part," Rockland responded. "*Colchicum autumnale* — that's the autumn crocus. Multiple species of rhododendron, barberry, gaillardia, dicentra, eucalyptus, buckthorn, bougainvillea, asclepias — that's the butterfly weed — lobelia, agave, cestrum, clematis, clivia, iris, euonymus, gladiolus, philodendron, juniperus, euphorbia, narcissus, cyclamen, chrysanthemum, delphinium, dieffenbachia and hydrangea. Did I mention *kalmia latisfolio*, mountain laurel, and *lantana camera?* Let's not overlook the leaves and stems of the nightshades, such as tomatoes. Of course, there are many other examples."

"I'm surprised gardening hasn't been banned," Cummings said, a bit stunned.

"Why? It's safe as long as one wears gloves and doesn't munch one's way through one's flower beds. How are things going in New England?"

"All right, I suppose. No breakthroughs. And in Chicago?

"The same. Nothing to report."

"I'll phone in a few days."

Cummings made another call, this time the promised call to his father. He dutifully made arrangements to visit that evening. That done, he had no other action items for the day. He decided to take a walk around Samaria.

The village looked much the same as it had when he lived in Maine. Maine changed slowly. Over a number of years one might notice fewer farms and less wooded land, more cheap and ugly houses and, in the coastal communities, more and better restaurants. But otherwise, Maine was Maine.

A farmers market was in progress in the town common, and Cummings wandered through it. The produce was hearty, and the crafts were perfunctory, though his attention was drawn to one vendor selling elegant candles.

"My mother and I make these the way our family's done for more than two hundred years," the vendor explained. He was a portly, middle-aged man with a beard. Apparently he had typed Cummings as a tourist from Boston or New York who might be impressed by such homespun salesmanship.

"Doesn't that make it difficult to turn a profit?" Cummings responded.

"You know what they say, anything worth doing ..." the man responded. "Besides, it's more of a hobby than anything else."

"What do you do the rest of the time?"

"I work in a factory."

Cummings bought several pairs of candles and moved on.

At the end of the farmers market, he saw that a crafts shop featuring the work of local artisans had opened. He browsed through it, perusing its crocheted oven mitts, corn husk dolls, wooden lobsters, dried soup mixes and scarves knitted from the wool of local sheep. Nothing caught his fancy. He returned to Horeb and took a long nap.

Coastal Maine is characterized by many inlets and peninsulas. Orchid and George, Cummings's father and stepmother, lived at the end of one in a village called Shiloh. Shiloh was about an hour's drive from Horeb along the corkscrew-shaped Shiloh Road. This wound through forest and pasture for about thirty miles south from Route 1, the main coastal highway. The only other way in was by the sea.

Shiloh was one of the many quaint, charming Maine villages with a mix of eighteenth century homes and twenty-first century gift shops. It was rumored that the Vikings may have landed nearby in the tenth century, and tourists have been spending their summers there for many of the years since.

Orchid had bought the house many decades and husbands ago, when coastal cottages with seaside acreage could be had cheap. The house was not impressive. It was a cedar-shingled fisherman's saltbox, built at some point in the nineteenth century and modernized over time. It was small: a kitchen, dining room, living room, two baths and three bedrooms, two of which were tiny.

However, the house sat on almost ten waterfront acres facing the Sheepscot Bay at the edge of an inlet known as Discord Harbor. The lot was a very long rectangle, only about three hundred feet wide. The house was reached by a very long, steep driveway off a leafy byway that forked off Shiloh Road. This had once led to a dairy farm and was called Whey Way. Who says New Englanders don't have a sense of humor?

There was a long, grassy decline that led from the house to a crag on the sea, a rocky cliff perhaps thirty feet above the waterline, which ran the width of the property. Worn wooden steps led from the edge of the grass down to a boat dock. This was not presently in use, as Orchid and George weren't particularly aquatic. Old stands of trees on both sides of the property separated the land from its neighbors.

Large flower and vegetable beds adorned each side of the house. Behind the house about half an acre was fenced. This area, reached through a gate near the end of the driveway, contained a small strip of lawn and a larger wooden deck. This was connected to the kitchen via sliders. These sliders served as the back door, and thus primary entrance, to the house.

Cummings walked through the gate and knocked on the sliders. George appeared and opened the door. George looked just as he always did: short, gaunt, crumpled and chaotic. In this respect he looked something like Albert Einstein, at least a thinner Albert Einstein. Also, there was George's madras.

George never wore anything but a madras bow tie over a wrinkled, white button-down shirt, with short or long madras pants and a madras blazer. Naturally, all of the madras patterns clashed. This blazer was one of George's three coats, the lightest in weight and often worn during the summer. He also owned an ancient, ill-fitting Harris Tweed, which he wore when colder temperatures prevailed and often when they didn't. Finally, he possessed a frayed herringbone sports jacket that dated to the 1970s.

"How are you, Dad?"

"Zesty."

"I'm glad, Dad. Are you and Orchid hungry? I thought I might take you out to dinner," Cummings asked, "or we could get some lobsters."

"Doesn't that require a boat?"

"I meant at the supermarket."

"Do you find me odd?" George asked suddenly but with his usual dispassion.

"What?" Cummings said, not expecting that question.

"Do you find me odd? Orchid says I'm odd."

"I think it's all relative," Cummings said tactfully. "One has to find individuals who share one's worldview."

"*Weltanschauung*. Fourteen letters. German."

"Exactly."

They headed toward the kitchen. As they did so George said, "Did you know Maine has thirty-three thousand, two hundred fifteen square miles; six thousand lakes and ponds; thirty-five hundred miles of coastline and seventeen million acres of forest?"

"No, I didn't," Cummings replied.

Orchid, Cummings's eighty-year-old stepmother, stood in the kitchen, sifting a large quantity of flour. She was small but taut, the probable result of a lifetime of physical vigor and intellectual athleticism. When Cummings had first met her years earlier, she'd had a long white ponytail. For reasons Cummings did not understand, and he didn't understand much about her, she had shaved her head for her wedding to his father. Her hair had grown back to haphazardly trimmed chaos. She wore jeans, a flannel shirt and slippers.

"Well, well, Cummings Flynn, Mister Repartee Rapier," Orchid said, looking up.

Cummings was surprised. Usually, she referred to him as "buddy" or "buddy boy."

"Hello, Orchid. How are you?"

"*Sain pour quelqu'un chancelant dans la tombe.*"

"Orchid, as you know, I don't speak French."

"I said I'm healthy for someone tottering into the grave. You should speak French. As my father used to say, if everyone spoke two or three languages, supper would have more discourses. I have studied nine different languages: English, French, German, Italian, Spanish, Urdu, Tamil, Chinese and Chichewa."

"I know, Orchid."

"Where is Chichewa spoken?"

"I don't have any idea."

"South Central Africa. I didn't think you'd know that. Where is Tamil spoken?"

"It's an Indian language, isn't it?" Cummings replied.

"Very good. There may be hope for you. I am making pies for the church bake sale. *Gehen Sie die Tortekrusten bilden!* I put the flour and the butter out on the counter. There are aprons over there in the broom closet."

"I don't know how to make *Tortekrusten*," Cummings, who did manage a little German in high school, replied.

"Nothing to it! I'll instruct you."

Some time later fifteen baked pie shells cooled on racks, waiting for filling. Chocolate cream, banana cream and custard cream fillings had been prepared, and blueberry filling heated on the stove. While Cummings stirred, Orchid lectured on various topics, such as the flora and fauna of Maine, the etymology of the word "goat," and the penis size of male nudes in Etruscan pottery. George sat nearby, working on puzzles, occasionally lifting his head to ask Cummings for assistance.

"I made up the guest room for you," Orchid announced as she finally transitioned from pies to dinner. Cummings checked the time on his phone. It was almost nine-thirty.

"Thank you, but I don't need it. I'm staying with Ernestine Cutter."

"Very well. Did I read something in the newspaper about a murder on her land?"

"Yes, but she had nothing to do with it."

"I assumed that, or you wouldn't be staying with her. If I remember correctly, a body was found in her boat."

"It wasn't her boat. She was just storing it for a friend, Deuteronomy Smelt."

"I don't know that name."

"He's a writer. Spy novels."

"That's right. I remember now. The Greek woman keeps house for him."

"You know them?"

"No. She's a friend of a friend of someone in our congregation. A few months ago the Greek woman came to our church and gave a little talk during coffee hour."

"About what?"

"She wants to open a Greek restaurant in Portland. She's looking for investors."

"How was the presentation?"

"Poorly conceived. She's a cook, not a businesswoman."

"Did anyone invest?"

"How should I know?"

Dinner was eventually cooked and eaten. Cummings helped to wash the dishes and left. By this time it was after midnight.

The next morning Cummings did not get up early. Late in the morning he returned to the old brick warehouse that housed Chess's orgone box factory. This time the factory was open for business, and he walked in the door.

Trying to be as inconspicuous as possible, Cummings circumnavigated the space, observing what he could. The main work area looked much the same as it had by flashlight, though it was easier now to take in its totality. The factory was busy, noisy and crowded. Workers in protective gear worked with concentration at the various machines, while their colleagues used hand tools to finish elements of the orgone boxes or to construct the final product. At one end completed orgone boxes, which looked something like small outhouses, were being crated for shipping.

He moved toward the office. The door was shut, and he knocked on it.

"Come right in," a cheerful male voice said from behind the door. Cummings opened it and entered.

The office remained in circumstances similar to Cummings's previous visit. The orderly section of the office remained tidy, and the section containing Chess's personal items seemed to have been untouched.

A man in his early thirties, wearing horn-rim glasses and a smart suit, white shirt and bow tie, sat behind the desk. He was reading a stack of papers as Cummings entered.

"It's as if two people inhabit this office," Cummings said playfully, referring to the mix of order and chaos.

The man laughed nervously. "I'm afraid the owner of our company died unexpectedly. We thought it best not to disturb his belongings, but, of course, work must go on."

"I'm so sorry to hear that," Cummings said.

"I'm Henry Nicholas," the man replied, rising and extending his hand. He smiled with the smooth ebullience of a successful salesman.

"Cummings Flynn Wanamaker."

"What can I do for you, Mister Wanamaker? Please sit down."

"I'm interested in purchasing an orgone box," Cummings said, sitting. "Are you the acting CEO, Mister Nicholas?"

"I'm the CFO. We're still working through what the transition will look like. Have you seen our brochure? There are a number of options." He removed a glossy publication from a file drawer and thrust it at Cummings.

"I've reviewed your website," Cummings said, "but I have a few questions." He made up a few and received a few answers. In between, he tried to ask casually about the state of the business: How long had Mister Nicholas been with the company? Had Chess been the sole owner, or had there been investors? Had the business been sold?

Mister Nicholas politely deflected Cummings's inquiries, and Cummings left a few minutes later with very little concrete information. Further, he had no intuitive sense whether Mister Nicholas was trying to project positivity in the face of unclear circumstances or trying to deflect unwanted questions to avoid revealing perfidious activities.

As he walked out of the office, he noticed the door to the lunch room was open. He glanced inside and saw three men sitting at a table, joking, drinking coffee and eating donuts. One he recognized as the chubby, bearded man who sold him candles the previous day in Samaria. Cummings invited himself into the room.

"I think we met yesterday," Cummings said, approaching the table. It took the man a few moments to recognize Cummings. "I bought some candles from you. I'm Cummings Flynn Wanamaker, by the way." Cummings extended his hand.

"That's right. You did. I'm John Harpwater," the man responded. He shook Cummings's hand. "This here is Glenn Marvell and Pauly Bolduc."

Hands were shaken all around.

"What are you doing here?" John asked Cummings. "In the market for an orgone accumulator, are you?"

"Yes, as a matter of fact."

"You've come to the right place. We make some wicked nice ones."

"So Mister Nicholas tells me. Incidentally, I'm so sorry to hear about your boss."

"Yes. Wicked bad thing. Wicked bad," John said, seemingly quite sad about Chess's death. His colleagues appeared to be similarly morose.

"Mister Nicholas said no decisions have been made about the business."

"That's what they tell us," John replied.

Cummings probed further, asking John and his friends questions similar to those he'd asked Mister Nicholas. The workers were even less forthcoming than the CFO.

Cummings was offered a maple walnut donut. He left the factory munching on it, feeling frustrated and wondering if an alternate path of inquiry would be more likely to advance his investigations. But what might it be?

Fifteen

At five-thirty the next morning Cummings received a call from Elektra.

"Mister Deuty wish you come at seven of the clocks. I make the Greek breakfast."

"Okay," Cummings said, yawning. He got out of bed and took a shower.

At a few minutes before seven, he approached the Smelt residence, where he observed Elektra in the yard, milking a goat. She gingerly squeezed the teats, resulting in exuberant bursts of liquid that she caught in a white plastic bucket. With her other hand, she was clutching a copy of Gypsy Rose Lee's novel, *The G String Murders*. Elektra appeared to be reading avidly.

"You here early, Mister Cummings," she said, a bit irritated. "I make teas, yogurts, fruits and *paximathaki* but not done yet."

"You shouldn't have gone to such trouble," he said, navigating around a large wheelbarrow that stood in his path.

"This not trouble. The Ottomans, that is trouble! The Greeks they say the good life is good food, good love and good revenge."

Cummings smiled.

"I understand you're thinking of opening a restaurant," he said.

"Who says this?"

"My stepmother. Apparently you made a presentation at her church."

"One day maybe. This is my dream. Okay, I finish breakfast. You into house and sit in parlor," she ordered. "Mister Deuty out soon from water closet."

Cummings went into the house. A few minutes later Deuteronomy emerged from his bedroom. In his pale tweed coat and subdued bow tie, he looked like a black-and-white author photograph from a 1950s book jacket. He sat down near Cummings.

Elektra, carrying a tray, entered the room, set it on a side table and then quickly left.

"It's good to see you," Cummings said. "You look well."

"Thank you," Deuteronomy replied. "I'm glad for this opportunity to exchange information. Please. Help yourself."

They ate and continued to chat.

"Has something happened? My impression was that you were eager to see me."

"It may well be that something has, but I can't be completely certain," Deuteronomy replied. "If I'm right, the implications are rather startling."

"What do you mean?"

"It's rather involved. Perhaps it might make more sense for you to update me first."

"All right. As I told you last time we met, I've been investigating Chess's death. However, I've also been looking into a murder in Chicago. I didn't mention this earlier because I had no reason to think there was any link between them."

"But you do now?"

"I think it's possible. The victim in Chicago was once married to Chess. Her name was Therese Hickok."

"One of the Hickok girls? You don't say! I didn't know Chess was ever married."

"Apparently the union was brief. They were both quite young. So you knew her?"

"A bit. This is a rural place, low population density. Everyone knows everyone. I did hear she'd passed on. I read it in the newspaper, I think, but I don't recall any details. How did she die?"

"She was giving a presentation to an occult group in Chicago and burned to death. It was made to look like spontaneous combustion."

"Is there some similarity to Chess's death — I refer to the manner of the crime — or other information that leads you to suspect the killer of both is the same?"

"No."

"But you've learned other information that's made you suspicious?"

"I'm suspicious because they were both murdered and within a few months of each other. They'd been married. There's also the connection with Wilhelm Reich. Therese wrote a book about Wilhelm Reich, and Chess manufactured orgone boxes. Of course, I don't know that necessarily means anything beyond a shared interest."

"We know that Chess wanted to write a book about the Cold War. Did Therese share that interest?"

"If she did, I don't know about it. I've investigated the members of the Mathers Society. That's the group Therese was speaking to when she died. They're harmless and eccentric. At least that's how they seem, though some are obviously withholding information. All of them had opportunity, most of them had the means, and some of them had a motive; but I don't have proof of anything or even much concrete suspicion. Also, there's a strange piece of jewelry that may have something to do with the crime, but I don't know what.

"As to Chess, there is even more lack of clarity. He seems to have been very popular; no one I'm aware of had an apparent reason to kill him. So that's all I know. I'm hoping you've learned more than I have."

"I have a theory about Chess's murder," Deuteronomy said. "It may seem a bit far-fetched, but hear me out. Do you recall that when we last met, I told you I needed to review some files?"

"Yes."

"I created these files over the years to track famous unsolved mysteries from the Cold War: the theft of state secrets, political assassinations, that sort of thing. I thought I might ultimately incorporate some of these tidbits into plots. When I saw Chess's notes for his book, it jogged my memory of a particular case, an unsolved assassination. The victim was a Polish writer named Wolfgang Babka. He defected to the West in the late 1960s, where he became something of an anti-Communist public intellectual. Have you heard of the case?"

"No," Cummings said, "but the Cold War isn't my bailiwick."

"The Communists made three attempts to kill Mister Babka. They finally succeeded in September of 1978. Babka was waiting at a London bus stop when he felt a slight pain on the back of his right thigh. He said it was like an insect bite. He looked around and saw a man pick up an umbrella off the ground, then scurry across the street. Babka described the umbrella as black and nondescript, the classic cane type—you know, the full-size umbrella that one might expect an English gentlemen to carry on a drizzly day. The man got into a taxi and drove off. Babka died a few days later."

"Do you think this has something to do with Chess?" Cummings asked.

"I'm getting to that," Deuteronomy said. "An autopsy revealed that the cause of Babka's death was ricin, a highly toxic poison. It was injected into Babka's thigh in a tiny metal pellet. The common view among those who think about such things is that it was likely delivered through a small injection gun embedded in that umbrella. Of course, no one's ever proved that, and the umbrella's never been recovered."

"I see," Cummings said to be polite. In truth, he did not see where Deuteronomy might be going with this.

"You may recall that while you were at Omurtag Farm, you ran into Howard Oliver," Deuteronomy continued. "You may also recall that he told you about a shipment of umbrellas from Eastern Europe."

"Of course," Cummings said, suddenly getting it. "You don't mean you think the umbrella in question somehow ended up in that silly museum?"

"Espionage is a nasty business. The umbrella was an unfortunate and embarrassing leftover of the Cold War. I think of these things as the dangling participles of espionage, silly mistakes that shouldn't have happened and now must be corrected. We know from his notes that Chess was going to write about the Babka case. Perhaps Chess somehow found out the umbrella was in the Museum."

"Someone killed him because he found the umbrella?"

"It's possible, isn't it?"

"Almost anything is, I suppose." In truth, Cummings was unconvinced. The proposition was too extraordinary. In Cummings's experience, murder was mundane, not prone to the eccentricities of spy fiction. He considered how to respond diplomatically.

"How would we determine if your theory is correct?" Cummings asked.

"We could have any umbrellas in the museum matching Babka's description of the murder weapon tested for ricin."

"And how would we manage that?"

Deuteronomy thought for a moment, then said, "I don't see how we would."

"In any case," Cummings said, "your theory doesn't explain why Chess's body was left in your boat, where it was sure to be discovered."

"I've thought about that. The location of the body almost guaranteed it wouldn't be discovered for months. This ensured deterioration that would mask the circumstances of the crime. Or it could have been a ruse to hide the real motive for the crime."

"Why would that be necessary?" Cummings asked, confused.

"I don't know yet. However, I suspect the idea may have been inspired by one of my novels, *Cat and Spouse,* published, as I recall, in 1962. In my book the villain, a KGB agent, planted a body in a rowboat as a diversion. A husband and wife spy team found the body. This distracted them temporarily from what was really going on, a plot to blow up the Hermitage. You see, one of the galleries concealed an underground vault in which smuggled United States military documents were hidden."

"That sounds like a James Bond movie."

"It was made into a movie, but unfortunately, it didn't involve 007 or anything else of interest," Deuteronomy sighed. "It was directed by a pompous auteur dope fiend just out of UCLA film school. Mercifully, the film was only released to drive-ins in the Midwest."

"Interesting, but as you said, there's no reasonable way to try and prove your theory."

Deuteronomy handed him a manila folder stuffed with newspaper clippings and handwritten notes.

"This is my file on the Babka case. Why don't you read through it? Maybe I've overlooked something. You could also make a trip to the Gethsemane Public Library. When I looked previously I didn't see much of use in their collection, but who knows? I might have missed something. Also, I don't bother with computers, so you might check the Web. Perhaps there's something in the electronic ether about the Babka case."

"I suppose I could follow up," Cummings agreed half-heartedly, "if you really think it's necessary."

"And don't forget to have a look see at the Museum. Interview Howard Oliver."

Reluctantly, Cummings was at the Gethsemane Public Library when it opened a few hours later. Gethsemane, about ten miles away, was the nearest town of any size to Horeb. Cummings carefully reviewed each item in Deuteronomy's folder, as well as the library's print and online resources. While he learned some additional details about the Babka murder, none of them involved the murder weapon or anything else of apparent relevance to Chess's demise.

This portion of his commitment to Deuteronomy fulfilled, he moved forward to complete the rest: he phoned Howard Oliver at the Ephemera Museum and made an appointment to see him after lunch.

Although it stood next to the Horeb Arts Center, housed in an imposing Victorian brick structure that had once been the village Grange Hall, the building housing the Ephemera Museum lacked distinction. The structure was a perfunctory metal warehouse built in the 1950s to store the trucks, sand and salt needed to make the roads in and around Horeb passable during the winter. These items had been moved to a larger warehouse in the early 1970s. Howard Oliver had been able to petition the board of selectmen successfully to purchase the old warehouse for one dollar. With minimal renovation, he had made it into a museum of objects of no value or interest — which, to the extent that anything Howard Oliver did had an objective, was probably the objective.

As Cummings walked up to the building's main door, he noticed an awkwardly lettered sign thumbtacked to the facade. This advertised the museum's current exhibition, "Toothpicks of the Americas." Cummings opened the door, which was in need of paint, and went in.

The interior was rudimentary: whitewashed steel beams and metal panel walls with a poured concrete floor, badly stained but at least level and not excessively cracked. A long partition, about six feet high, separated the lobby area from the exhibition space behind it. A cheap desk and several chairs were positioned in front, presumably to greet visitors and take admission fees. At one end of the space a gift shop area had been created. This offered local artisanal items from metal bins on metal shelving.

Howard Oliver sat at the desk reading a Superman comic book.

"Cummings!" Howard said enthusiastically, looking up as Cummings entered the space. "How nice to see you! Welcome to the Maine Ephemera Museum."

"Thank you, Howard," Cummings replied.

"Have you visited us before?" Howard asked.

"I don't believe so."

"Let me give you the tour."

They started in the toothpick exhibition. This involved various examples of the toothpick makers' art from woods indigenous to different places in the Western Hemisphere. Each artifact was carefully arranged on white china placed atop white pedestals. Howard slowly explained the provenance of each toothpick, resulting in the most boring thirty-seven minutes Cummings had ever experienced.

Finally they emerged from toothpick purgatory and walked past another partition into the permanent exhibit: umbrella covers. These were pinned to cork boards mounted at eye level. Howard's narration continued.

The umbrella covers that Howard had mentioned at Omurtag Farm all seemed to be displayed. They ranged in color from faded red to dirty beige to worn gray, but no black. Further, there appeared to be only one umbrella from England or thereabouts, and it was a Burberry plaid.

"Your interest is only the covers, not the actual umbrellas? Is that correct?" Cummings asked.

"Yes. We keep the covers and dispose of the umbrellas."

"How do you dispose of them?"

"I give them to Genevieve Bolduc. Do you know Genevieve? A very talented craftsperson! She uses the umbrella skins to make grocery bags and recycles the aluminum into garden ornaments."

"Do all of your umbrellas come in as donations? For example, from the proprietors of Omurtag Farm?"

"Yes. That's exactly what happens."

"Do you keep records? Who donated what? Where each umbrella was manufactured?"

"Well, we try. Truthfully, recordkeeping isn't my strength. I'm more of an inspiration person."

"And this is the entire collection? Everything is on display?"

"Well, no, not all of it," Howard replied. "Genevieve usually helps me clean and mount the new umbrella covers as they come in, but she had a baby about six months ago. I haven't seen much of her. There's quite a backlog of umbrellas waiting in our storage room."

"Can I see those?"

"I don't see why not."

They walked to the back of the warehouse, and Howard unlocked a door. The store room was lined with steel shelves on which were piled umbrellas of every color, size and shape. Cummings did his best to look through them and noticed at least a dozen that matched the general description of the Babka murder weapon.

"Where are these from?"

"All sorts of places."

"Are any from Eastern Europe or the United Kingdom?"

"Some might be."

"Do you know which ones?"

"Like I said, I'm not much on recordkeeping."

Sometime after midnight Cummings was awakened by a commotion too loud to ignore. He got out of bed and looked out his window. The sky was illuminated and smoky. A building was on fire in the village.

He dressed quickly and went downstairs. There he found Ernestine in her bathrobe.

"Do you know what's going on?" Cummings asked.

"There's a fire. Don't you smell it?" she responded.

Cummings nodded and left the house.

Walking to the village center, Cummings saw the Horeb volunteer fire department, as well as volunteer firemen from three surrounding communities, rushing toward the Maine Ephemera Museum. The Museum was a mass of flames.

A number of townsfolk stood watching in dismay. One of them was Deuteronomy.

"What happened?" Cummings asked, approaching him.

"No one really knows," Deuteronomy said. "The building just started to burn."

"Any idea of the cause?" Cummings asked.

"Who can say? They heated the place with propane. Perhaps the tank exploded. Perhaps it was something in the wiring. I doubt Howard's done much updating. Or it could be arson."

"Isn't arson a rather extreme solution? Even if the Babka umbrella was in there, why go to all the trouble of setting the building on fire? Surely such evidence would never be discovered. We're talking about an eccentric museum in a tiny village in Maine that is visited by almost no one."

"Do you recall what I said about dangling participles? The CIA doesn't like them," Deuteronomy said, "and neither does the KGB."

"Yes, but surely ..." Cummings saw from Deuteronomy's expression there was little point in continuing the sentence, let alone the conversation. Deuteronomy's mind was made up.

They stood together in silence, watching the blaze for a long time. Shortly after dawn Elektra came for Deuteronomy and took him back to his house. Cummings went back to Ernestine's and made some tea. He sipped it thoughtfully.

Sixteen

Cummings returned to Chicago just in time for the Fourth of July. Cummings and Odin got up early and drove toward the center of Illinois to spend the day with Odin's sister, Rosaline.

Odin's parents were gone as the result of a car accident, and Rosaline was his only living sibling. "It's important to keep those family ties knotted," Odin liked to say. Cummings was never sure if this meant that intimacy should be maintained with one's biological family at all costs or that all family connections were inherently tangled. Whichever, Odin felt a need to see Rosaline occasionally. Cummings, as a good spouse, went along.

About two and a half hours south of Chicago, Odin turned off the highway to a secondary road. Some minutes later he veered onto a tertiary road, then another even more tertiary. Finally he turned onto a bumpy and dusty dirt road slicing through densely planted corn fields.

Eventually the corn parted, revealing a worn Victorian farm house with an adjacent barn surrounded by acres of prairie grasses. A winding gravel driveway led from the road to the house, passing a neatly fenced vegetable garden that appeared well tended and fecund.

Several dogs ran toward the approaching car, barking, as a sturdy middle-aged woman with her hair in pigtails came out of the house. She was tall but much stockier than Odin, though her facial features were similar enough that one might easily deduce they were related.

"You found your way," she said flatly as Odin and Cummings emerged from the car. "Thought I might get a call saying you were lost."

"I remember how to get here," Odin replied.

She nodded. "Come in then," she said, turning toward the house.

As he always did, Cummings scanned her waist to see what kind of gun she was carrying. It wasn't that he was concerned his sister-in-law would kill him; it was the reassurance of observing natural order. As surely as the sun rose and set on a schedule, Rosaline got up every morning and put on a gun. They were her totems. This particular afternoon, a .45 was holstered around her midriff and jiggled menacingly as she walked.

Inside, the house was comfortable and cozy. The room was painted a light gold color with a medley of throw pillows in florals, stripes and patterns strewn randomly on old and shabby overstuffed furniture. Four leaf-patterned dog beds lay at the compass points of the room; one was next to an old and shabby gun rack, overstuffed with firearms. Cummings was pleased to note there was a padlock on it.

Rosaline made lemonade, which she brought out in a pitcher with mismatched glasses.

"We're very shabby chic around here," she said, putting the drinks down on a side table. "Help yourselves." She plopped into a side chair, put her cowboy-booted feet up on the table and picked up some knitting from a wicker basket on the floor.

"What are you making?" Cummings asked.

"Piggy socks for my little piggies," she said, snorting and showing a half finished sock to Cummings. It was pink with a striped motif of alternating pigs feet and pigs tails. "I like piggies. Thought about starting a hog farm, but it's too messy.

The runoff's poison. It'll make you sicker than the government."

"I have a new job," Odin said, changing the subject. "Product testing. It's only temporary and part-time, but they might hire me full-time."

"What are you testing?"

"Tampon strength, the water tightness of disposable diapers, that sort of thing."

"I thought you did something with computers," she said.

"I'm using my engineering degree," Odin said defensively. "They also test other products. Tires, for example. This could lead to something better."

"Did you hear that we bought that old warehouse building in Blue Mound?" Rosaline asked.

"No, I don't think you told us," Odin replied.

"It was real cheap, and I thought we might make some money renting it out. Some people turned up and said they wanted to put in a day care center, so we leased them the place. They paid their rent on time, but after a while Baxter noticed there weren't no children. So I went over there. It was a meth lab. I had to call the Illinois Watchmen of Freedom to get them out."

"Did you lose a lot of money?" Odin asked.

"Hell, no. I started a business."

"What kind of business?"

"I'll show you." She ran upstairs and returned with several furry doll heads in the shapes of various animals.

"Stuffed animals?" Cummings guessed.

"Not exactly. We put them on carry bags. Their little heads just pop over the top of the bag. We make a doggie bag, and a kitty carry all and a bunny bag and a tiger tote. And see, they all have little pockets for hand guns. Aren't they cute?

Little girls love them. I have them in stores all over Central and Southern Illinois."

"That's impressive," Odin said.

Rosaline sat. There was a pause in the conversation, then she said to Cummings, "You're from Maine, aren't you?"

"I lived there for a while," Cummings replied.

"Do you know the Maine Sons of Liberty militia?" she inquired.

"I don't believe so," Cummings said.

"My friends moved up there, Grant and Betsy Jackson. You remember them, Odin?"

"Abraham Jackson's younger brother," Odin said. "Wasn't he in prison?"

"No. The government dropped the sedition charges. You guys shoot? Come down here and hunt when you like," she said cheerfully. "The land's still half yours, Odin."

"We're not much on hunting," Odin said.

"Must be something to hunt in Chicago. The mayor, to start. You know, we have almost two thousand acres here," she said to Cummings. "I've been letting the Illinois Patriot Militia do weekend maneuvers."

"How are Baxter and Parker?" Odin asked, changing the subject again. He was referring to his nephews.

"Fine, just fine. They're supposed to be home any minute."

As if on cue, Cummings heard a door open. This was followed by some mumbling and heavy footfall, as if a large animal was lumbering into the house. A few seconds later, two males appeared, one about Rosaline's age and another, a lanky teenager with a small amount of acne and a large football helmet. The teenager had his arm around the older man, supporting him.

"I can walk just fine," the man said, sloppy drunk, trying to push the teenager away.

"Maybe, maybe not," the teenager snapped back. They headed toward the stairs.

"Damn, if we weren't just talking about you," Rosaline said. "Moab, where have you been?"

"I got to take a nap," the man mumbled in response, hanging onto the stair rails as he hoisted himself along. The teen returned after delivering his burden to the bedroom. He plopped down into a chair and took off his football helmet.

"Hello, Baxter," Odin said, awkwardly extending his hand to shake. "You remember your Uncle Cummings."

"Haven't seen you for a while," Baxter observed.

"Not since Christmas," Odin responded.

"There's some lemonade," Rosaline said, pointing. "There's more in the refrigerator. Where was your father?"

"He was heading to Cousin Mike's."

"That's Moab's drinking buddy," Rosaline said, mostly for Cummings's benefit. "We think he sells heroin."

"How did you know where he was going?" Cummings asked.

"I got him on GPS," Baxter replied proudly. "I bought a tiny transmitter and super glued it into his wallet. So now, any time he goes on a bender, I just track him and pick him up in my truck."

Delighted laughter exploded out of Baxter, and his mother started laughing, too.

"He's smart like you," she guffawed, smacking Baxter on the side of the head affectionately. She looked at Cummings and Odin and asked, "Either of you want some Jack in your lemonade?"

"Jack" referred to Jack Daniels whiskey, of which Rosaline was quite a fan. Rosaline and Cummings had several servings. Odin abstained, as he was driving.

During the drive home Cummings received a phone call from Winky Carmello.

"I'm afraid the police think Crandall killed Therese," Winky exclaimed.

"Has he been arrested?"

"No, but they've been here twice. They just left. He doesn't know I'm phoning you. He thinks I'm overreacting. They said they found bee stuff at the crime scene."

"Traces of beeswax?"

"That's it. They think it came from Crandall's hives."

"That's not compelling evidence. Bees are common. So are beehives. I don't think you have much to worry about, at least not now. However, I do have a question for you. Did you invite Tom to go to the auction with you, the one I saw you at a few weeks ago?"

"No. I just ran into him there."

"I see."

"How are you coming with your investigation?"

"It's going slowly."

"Does that mean you don't know who killed Therese yet?"

"That's correct," Cummings conceded, "but I'm working on it."

A few minutes later Rockland phoned.

"Where are you two?" Rockland asked.

"Driving back to Chicago from Odin's sister."

"Did she shoot you?"

"Fortunately, no."

"Do you want to come for drinks tomorrow?"

"I don't see why not. What are you two doing?"

"Luther and I are having our traditional Fourth of July celebration," Rockland said with marked sarcasm. "Right now we're raising our mint juleps to the Dred Scott decision. Later I'm going to do a dramatic reading of the Indian Removal Act of 1830."

"I thought you were going on a picnic."

"It was cancelled. We were going with another couple, two of Luther's colleagues from the music department. One of them has a cold."

"Do you recall that I smelled a rather sharp odor before the fire at the Mathers meeting?" Cummings said. "Did I mention it had a slightly fragrant quality? Perhaps it was beeswax. What do you think?"

"It's difficult to say," Rockland responded. "It's possible the accelerant was linseed oil mixed with something. It's also possible the accelerant contained no linseed oil at all. However, the combination of beeswax and linseed oil doesn't make sense. Beeswax wouldn't contribute chemically to enhance the flammability or in any other way that I can think of. So why add it?"

"Because not everyone's as smart as you are. Murderers make mistakes."

"The larger problem is that we don't have enough information to do more than speculate. Now if you could steal a copy of the arson investigation report from the Chicago Fire Department ..."

"I don't see how I could do that," Cummings said, "but I do know someone who might. Rutley Paik, you may recall, is a fireman."

"He's the former husband of the victim, right? Let me know if he's cooperative," Rockland replied. "Now before you go, I have something important to tell you."

"What?"

"Because our plans for today did not come off, I had free time this morning. As I told you I would keep an eye on Tom Daniels, I did some surveillance."

"Did something occur?"

"You could say that. I sat in my car in front of his house for more than an hour. I was parked in such a way that I had a clear line of sight to the door, though I couldn't hear much. A strange little man, rather troll-like, made an appearance."

"Mandrake. That must be Mandrake. He works for Otto."

"The troll-like creature banged on the door, and Daniels answered. Daniels wouldn't let the fellow into his home, so they talked on the porch. The body language suggested there was no love lost between these gentlemen. After a terse discussion Daniels angrily thrust a book at ... what did you say his name was? Mandrake?"

"That's right. Could you identify the book?"

"I'm getting to that. What I observed seems to confirm your description of the book, *The Chainmail Thong* or whatever it was, though I can't be absolutely certain. At a distance the tawdry colors seemed reminiscent of those silly gay romance novels that Luther is so fond of. Also, as you will see, it was definitely hollow.

"Instead of taking possession of the book when it was thrust at him, Mandrake clumsily dropped it. As it fell to the porch, it opened, and what appeared to be American currency flew out. I couldn't see the denominations. It appeared that the book had been carved out in its interior and the pages glued together, a sort of informal safe. There were a lot of bills. Mandrake hurriedly retrieved the cash and scurried off, and Daniels went back inside.

"Thus, in short, I saw a dubious transaction involving empty prose," Rockland concluded. "The question is, was this merely an aggressive variation on *The New York Times Book Review* or something more sinister?"

"Thank you, Rockland. You have no idea how helpful this information is!"

"Glad to be of service."

The first thing after the holiday weekend, Cummings made two calls. First he left a message for Rutley Paik, asking him to call, and then he phoned Otto and insisted they meet. Cummings requested that the meeting take place somewhere other than Otto's home and that Mandrake not be present. Otto seemed hesitant but ultimately agreed.

"Let's meet at the stairs in front of the Art Institute," Cummings suggested. Otto acceded. They set the meeting for noon. Cummings arrived a few minutes early, and Otto arrived a few minutes late. Barbara Cartland trotted beside him, tethered by a rhinestone-covered leash.

"We cannot talk here. It's far too noisy," Otto opined. "It's such a lovely day! Shall we find a bench in Millennium Park?"

They wandered into the park on the block behind the Art Institute and quickly located a bench under the shade of several ash trees.

"What are you so eager to speak with me about?" Otto asked as he sat. The day was warm and getting warmer. Otto removed a Japanese fan from his pocket, unfurled it languidly, and fanned himself. Barbara Cartland, panting, lay on the ground where it was cooler.

"I believe that Mandrake is blackmailing Tom Daniels and possibly you." Cummings watched Otto carefully as he said this. There was no apparent reaction.

"Why do you say that?" Otto asked flatly.

"Because Mandrake was observed taking a substantial cash payment from Tom Daniels."

"Why would you think Mandrake is blackmailing me?"

"That's obvious, isn't it? You claim you're being blackmailed. He works for you. He appears to be blackmailing a close friend of yours. They're even passing money in a hollow copy of one of your books."

"Which one?"

"*Love's Tender Chainmail.*"

"Not my best. I fear it's all a bit twee, particularly the donkey."

"You're like a squirrel that hides information rather than nuts," Cummings said, experiencing a rising sense of exasperation. "There are a number of matters you have promised to explain but haven't—for example, whatever you know about Mandrake's activities, which I suspect is a lot, though I can't prove it yet."

"I don't know a thing about it."

"You're lying, but we'll move on. Why won't you go to the police with the letters? What else do you know about the Mathers members? Why were you visiting a falsely convicted man in prison, and what, if anything, does that have to do with Therese's death?"

"I told you everything there is to tell about Edgar when we met in the prison. Honestly, I did," Otto insisted, with an anxious whine.

"It is time to tell me everything you're not telling me. Otherwise, I'm done with you. Further, I will go to the police and tell me them what little I've learned."

"Please, you can't do that!"

"Is Mandrake blackmailing Tom?"

"It's very complicated. Things are not as they appear to be. Don't go to the police."

"Is Mandrake blackmailing you?"

"Of course not. Please give me a few more days. I'll explain everything. Really, I will!"

"You've said that before."

"Please be patient with me! A few more days. That's all I ask!"

Otto stood suddenly, grasped Barbara Cartland's leash and walked forcefully in the direction of Michigan Avenue.

"Otto!" Cummings called after him, but it was no use. He didn't turn back.

Cummings sat for a few minutes, contemplating the paradoxes of Otto Verissimo. He was inscrutable and a liar. Did he know something about Therese's death? Was he protecting himself? From what or whom? Or possibly, was Otto like the heroes of his romance novels, sacrificing himself to protect someone else?

What of the blackmail? Was Mandrake extorting Tom? Was Otto trying to protect one or both of them? Could Mandrake be blackmailing Tom on Otto's behalf? Might Mandrake be working for someone other than Otto? And above all, why was Otto so hesitant to confide in Cummings, someone he'd hired to protect him?

On the way home Cummings made a visit to Tom Daniels. Tom, half-asleep, opened the door. His skin was still pallid, and he looked feverish.

"I'm sorry to turn up without calling first. I see that your cold appears to be lingering," Cummings said. "Are you well enough for a brief chat?"

"I have bronchitis. I was taking a nap."

"So sorry. I'll come another time."

"What do you want?"

"Just a few questions. You told me you were at the auction because Winky invited you to join him."

"Right."

"Winky says that's not true."

"There must be some misunderstanding."

"At the auction, I saw Mandrake give you a copy of *Love's Tender Chainmail*."

"Yes. He'd borrowed it. He was returning it."

"Why would he borrow your copy? Doesn't he have one of his own? If not, couldn't he borrow a copy from the author who is, after all, his employer?"

"Right. I know that seems odd, but nonetheless ..."

"A few days ago," Cummings continued "you gave Mandrake a great deal of money in a hollow copy of *Love's Tender Chainmail*. Is Mandrake, or someone Mandrake answers to, blackmailing you?"

Tom looked startled by the question. Cummings could see he was intellectually scrambling, likely trying to think of a convincing story that would allay Cummings's suspicions. "I'm sorry. I'm not feeling at all well. Perhaps it would be best ..."

"Speak to me, or speak to the police," Cummings interrupted.

"I don't have to speak to anyone," Tom insisted.

"I assume the reason you're being blackmailed is that you killed Therese Hickok. Or is there another reason?"

"I didn't kill anyone!" Tom declaimed.

"That may be true. I'll admit things don't quite add up. You don't have an obvious motive for murder. Otto doesn't have a motive for blackmail. You're old friends, and he has plenty of money without taking yours. Otto implied that Mandrake is not blackmailing you. Then again, it's difficult to know who is telling the truth and who isn't."

"Then let me help you — nothing you've said is remotely true!" Tom stated as forcefully as he could. "I have nothing else to say. Please leave now." Tom slammed the door shut.

Rutley didn't respond to Cummings's message. Cummings made several more attempts to reach him over the next few days. Rutley never answered his phone and didn't return the calls either. Cummings wasn't sure what to make of this. He finally drove to Rutley's home to leave a note.

As he approached the front door, he saw it was open. He went inside to discover a distraught Mary Collins, face covered with streaky makeup, the apparent result of a lengthy period of sobbing.

The living room in which they stood was a mess. The chaos was not so anarchic as to suggest that the home had been burglarized. Instead, the relative orderliness of piles of clean and dirty laundry, empty food containers, scattered papers, and accumulating dust suggested that the room hadn't been cleaned in a long time.

"Hello, Mary. I'm looking for Rutley. Is he here?"

"No," she said, bursting into tears.

"Has something happened?"

"He's dead," she explained in between sobs. "He was killed in a fire."

"What fire?"

"It happened last night. Somewhere on the South Side. Kids were shooting off Roman candles. He was trapped in the building or something."

"How do you know this?"

She retrieved a folded copy of the *Chicago Tribune* from her shoulder bag and handed it to him. "The story's on page four," she said.

Cummings perused the article, which was brief and added few additional facts. He considered what he knew. None of the Mathers members lived on the South Side of Chicago. Nothing in the *Tribune* article suggested a criminal aspect to the fire. Rutley's death was likely just common tragedy, the sort of thing that happens every day to first responders.

"I came over as soon as I read the paper," Mary explained tearfully as Cummings handed the newspaper back to her. "I thought perhaps I could be of some assistance. Notify family members. Do something."

"I suppose we could straighten up," Cummings said.

"Yes," Mary replied, slightly more cheerful. "At least whoever walks in next won't be walking into a mess."

"Right," Cummings agreed.

In truth, his motivation was not altruistic. During the almost two hours they spent neatly stacking papers, taking out trash, washing dishes, putting them away and returning recently laundered clothes to drawers, Cummings was on a hunt. Eventually he found what he was looking for: a copy of the Red and White arson investigation report. It was wedged between empty pizza cartons. The first page was stained—red wine and chocolate, Cummings guessed. Cummings surreptitiously folded the stapled sheets and put them in his back pocket.

Cummings offered Mary a lift. She declined. He returned to his car and read the report. Of course, it contributed nothing to his knowledge of Rutley's death; but as he'd hoped, it did add to what he knew about Therese's — added in a rather startling way. He considered the new information for a few moments, then settled on a course of action.

Using the GPS function on his smart phone, he searched for the nearest hardware store. On the drive over his phone rang.

"Cummings here," he answered.

"Things are at a very sensitive point," an irate Otto screeched. "Very sensitive! I told you that I'll tell you everything in a few days! How could you do this?"

"How could I do what?" Cummings replied calmly.

"Intimidate Tom Daniels! He's furious!"

"I didn't intimidate anyone. I asked him a few questions!"

"Don't you have any emotional intelligence?" Otto shrieked.

"I'm not sure what emotional intelligence is, so possibly not. Are you firing me?"

"No!"

"Good. In spite of what I may have implied in the park, I haven't quit either. You can expect my next bill shortly. Very well then. I'm in traffic. I'll phone you in a day or two." Cummings hung up.

At the hardware store Cummings searched the aisles, looking for a particular item. He picked it up and took it to the cash register.

Next he went home, and got onto his computer. After a brief search he found some evidence confirming his new suspicions: a twenty-year-old article from the *Chicago Sun-Times*.

Finally he phoned Clarkson's auction house.

"I wonder if you can help me," Cummings said. "I'm a bookkeeper. One of my clients has misplaced some paperwork she needs for her tax return. Could you look up something if I give you the client number? It's CB175. I'll be happy to confirm the name and address."

"That would be helpful."

Cummings stated the information.

Apparently, that convinced. The voice on the phone asked politely, "What would you like me to look up, sir?

Cummings responded, "I want to verify some of Mrs. Hollingbery's recent transactions."

Seventeen

A few days later, in the same morning edition, the *Chicago Tribune* published two articles of particular interest to Cummings. He found these tidbits comforting. He was feeling particularly frustrated by his relative lack of progress, and they reminded him that everything remaining unclear in his investigations would likely become clear in time.

One item was a brief article confirming the cause of the house fire in which two Chicago firemen, one of whom was Rutley Paik, had been killed: children shooting off fireworks. This was a confirmation of what Cummings had already assumed, that there was nothing sinister about Rutley's death.

The second bit of news was of even greater interest because it established the veracity of something Cummings had assumed was a lie. The District Attorney of Cook County announced that, based on new evidence, Edgar Diderot was going to be released from prison. Otto had been telling the truth, at least about Edgar. This did not, of course, necessarily mean Otto was telling the truth about anything else, but at least it took one paradox off Cummings's list.

Cummings dressed and drove to his first appointment, which was with Anunciación Hollingberry. She answered the door promptly after Cummings rang and ushered him into her living room.

"Thank you for seeing me," Cummings said.

"I always like to be helpful, don't you know." She led him to a chair and indicated he should sit. "Do you still think Surendra was murdered?"

"I'm afraid so."

"Not everything in the world is explainable by science! There are some matters that are beyond our comprehension!"

"Indeed, but I don't think this is one of them."

"We will have to agree to disagree." Anunciación sat. "You said you wanted to speak to me again?"

"Yes. I'd like to ask you about your interest in the Craddock Brooch."

"What do you mean?"

"You purchased it at auction."

"I did! My old friend Despina was very ill with heart trouble, and it was said the brooch had the power to heal. I bought it, took it to her home in Wales and placed it on her heart chakra. Sadly, it was no use. She passed anyway.

"Dear Despina! I knew her from the convent school in South Dakota, don't you know. She was called Muffin then, but she later married an Italian viscount with whom she lived in a ninth century tower on the Tiber. One can't live in a ninth century tower on the Tiber with a viscount and be called Muffin.

"Fellini used their home as a set in *Satyricon*. He gave them small roles in an orgy scene. There was a close-up of her nipples. Her husband's family was scandalized and cut off their money. They took what they had left, moved to Wales and began to raise sheep and carrots for better quality restaurants.

"Perhaps the plan was not completely thought through. Did you know the Welsh word for carrots is *moron?* That was Despina's pet name for the Viscount.

"I'm afraid they faced many difficulties: a flood, then a fire, unstable prices, and an outbreak of feedlot rectal prolapse — that's a sheep disease. But eventually ..."

"You purchased the Craddock Brooch at auction," Cummings interrupted, attempting to return Anunciación to the linear.

"Yes. That's right! It seems the brooch is only a worthless piece of costume jewelry carved from sheep bone. Who can say if it even belonged to Ida Craddock? I resold it at auction. I didn't know who bought it, though I suppose it now seems likely it was purchased by Therese."

"It was a gift from her husband, actually. You didn't tell Therese it was a fake?"

"I didn't know she was going to buy it, don't you know. But even if I had, I wouldn't have said anything. No matter how unfounded it is, one must never destroy hope. It is too scarce and too fragile."

"Speaking of auctions, you've sold a number of items, furniture mostly, during the last year. In fact, you sold something recently at Clarkson's."

"What if I have? I'm about to redo several rooms in my apartment."

"I wonder if there's another reason, that the financial downturn has been hard on you, as it has been on everyone who lives on investment income."

"I don't need money. I've been very fortunate, don't you know."

Cummings paused to survey the room. "Your furniture really is lovely."

"Thank you."

"But I must confess that I was confused by why a woman in your financial position had reproduction antiques," Cummings continued. "A few days ago I discovered the reason. This furniture was made by your late husband."

"That's true! How did you learn that?"

"I found an old article about him in the *Sun-Times,*" he said, unfolding a printout from his coat pocket and handing it to her. "Apparently your late husband relaxed from the stress of the Chicago Board of Trade by making furniture. It seems that he was quite the craftsman, even winning blue ribbons for his work. He also developed a polish for fine furniture, Heirloom Formula, that's still sold locally. In fact, I bought some yesterday at the hardware store. Its primary ingredients are beeswax and linseed oil, and it's scented with lavender."

"He was a remarkable man, at least when he was sober," Anunciación said wistfully. "I miss him."

"Did you know that the Chicago Fire Department determined that Heirloom Formula was the accelerant used to burn Therese to death?"

"That's not possible!"

"That's not to say I think you had anything to do with her death. You had no reason to kill her, at least that I'm aware of."

"Of course I didn't!"

"However, consider the following: Let's say you needed money badly. Perhaps you recognized your husband's product as the accelerant. You must be quite familiar with its odor and characteristics. Let's assume you also figured out who the murderer was. It appears that Tom Daniels, who is a trust fund baby, is being blackmailed, so let's assume he's the murderer."

"What are you trying to say?" she snapped, looking intently at him. Her eyes suggested a rising fury.

"That I think you're blackmailing Tom. Let's further assume that to distance yourself from the crime, you somehow coerced Mandrake to act as a go-between," Cummings continued. "Let's also suppose Otto found out about the blackmail and in his quirky way has been trying to find a way out of this predicament for both Mandrake and

Tom. That would explain why he brought me into the situation."

"You son of a bitch!" Anunciación shrieked in a hot Mediterranean rage. She rose from her chair, grabbed a small crystal bowl from a side table and hurled it at Cummings. It missed, shattering on the floor. "You think you're so clever! Why don't you know this?"

She threw open a drawer in a Chinese cabinet, pulled out a legal document and threw it at Cummings. It landed at his feet. He picked it up and perused it.

"This appears to be a contract," he said.

"Yes, you idiot!" she confirmed. "You are correct that I needed money. Proctor and Gamble has been dogging me for decades to buy Heirloom Formula. Things being how they are, I accepted their offer a few months ago for more money than you will ever see in your life! I had no reason to blackmail anyone!"

Cummings considered this. He also consulted the figure stipulated in the contract, which included many zeros. "I suppose it's possible I've miscalculated," he conceded finally.

"How could I do such a thing? With my sweet disposition!"

She picked up another small object, a Sandwich Glass decanter, and threw it at Cummings. It grazed him before landing safely on a sofa cushion.

"I apologize," Cummings said, rising hurriedly. "Perhaps you could stop throwing things at me now?"

"Out! Get out!"

Cummings made an athletic leap for the door, opened it and ran for the elevator.

By the time he came out of the lobby and was safely back on the street, his adrenalized condition was beginning to ebb.

Worse, he was feeling regretful, not about falsely accusing Anunciación but about making a significant error.

He sat in his car and considered, then reconsidered, all the facts that had led to his erroneous conclusion. He then considered the same facts again but with a focus on what other conclusions they might lead to. Suddenly he saw his mistake. There was another even stronger possibility, one that seemed not merely plausible but now appeared to be obvious.

When the mail came, Cummings was pleased to discover a substantial check from Otto. He immediately went to the bank and deposited it. Still, working for Otto was hardly steady income. He spent the bulk of the day following up another batch of leads for jobs and consulting work, something that had become a frequent and frustrating routine.

The most promising, which wasn't promising at all, was an inquiry from the Magen David Pet Cemetery. They wanted a consultant to assess why its requests for funding to the city's many philanthropies were uniformly being rejected.

"Perhaps they don't view it as a priority," Cummings suggested during a call with the Director.

"But we have an online bereavement group!" the Director insisted.

Later Cummings managed to create an informal but filling dinner for himself and Odin, who seemed glum when he came home from work.

"Did something happen today?"

"I was asked to test the tensile strength of aluminum-reinforced pantyhose. I didn't spend six years in school for this."

"Persevere."

"What's the point?"

"Have you heard anything from your job interview?"

"No."

"Things will improve. I have to go out for a few hours. Try and relax."

Odin nodded. He turned on the television, took his dinner to the sofa and stared blankly at the screen.

Boys Town, an area in and around ten blocks of North Halsted Street in Chicago's Lakeview neighborhood, is the city's historic gay and lesbian enclave. This designation, dating back to 1970, is acknowledged with place markers: eleven pairs of twenty-three-foot-high, slightly tapered phallic pillars with rings adorning them in the colors of the rainbow.

Boys Town has evolved in the last decades. The irony of social progress is that marginalization strengthens minority cultures while assimilation weakens them. In the post-gay world of the twenty-first century, Boys Town is no longer needed as a ghetto stronghold. A gay and lesbian presence remains, but Boys Town is a community now, not an enclave, and that community is diverse.

Boys Town was Cummings's destination for the evening. He wanted specifically to visit several businesses including two gay bars, though not for the beer and flirting.

Cummings found a place to park his car and walked to his first destination. This was a tavern called The Wicked Age, Chicago's oldest surviving gay bar, founded in 1927. It was named after a play written by and starring Mae West, an early gay rights supporter as well as an actress. *The New York Times* called the play "the low point of the theatrical season of

1927-1928," and the show closed after nineteen performances. The bar has fared better.

Like so many Chicago tavern interiors, it was dark and oaken. There was a long wooden bar, the walls were covered in wood paneling, and there were wood shutters on the windows. Curiously, the light fixtures were art deco layer cakes. The original owner, Louis Gager, commissioned these as a visual joke. *Cake eater* was slang for *homosexual* in the late 1920s.

Cummings walked in and looked around, surveying the surfaces, the clientele and their activities. Little was happening. There seemed to be few patrons, even for a week night, and they didn't seem a very lively bunch at that.

Cummings left and went to the second destination. This was a much newer bar, Cement Pond, a sawdust and plank floor burger joint that served two hundred varieties of obscure beer and featured drag queen waitresses dressed like Elly May Clampett. Cummings was surprised to discover that the place was closed, not just for the evening but for good. A handwritten sign taped in the window announced the venue had ceased operations three weeks earlier.

So far, it was as Cummings had theorized, but he wasn't certain his final stop would continue the trend.

He walked a few blocks to a small office building. It was locked up for the night. He assumed it would be, and that was fine. What he was looking for, if it was even there, wouldn't be in plain sight.

Looking through the front window, his choices were these: take the risk of breaking in and hope he found useful information, or dig through the trash and hope that useful information had been foolishly discarded. Neither option seemed promising, but worst case, digging in the trash was likelier to result in wasted time than a jail sentence. So the trash it was.

He walked to the immediate back of the building, where there were two large commercial dumpsters. He threw open the heavy metal lid of one and climbed inside with a flashlight.

As Rockland might have observed, contradicting Dostoyevsky, the one subject so old that nothing new can be said of it is trash. The refuse in this dumpster did as garbage has always done: it rotted, it slimed, it stank. Cummings persevered, carefully digging through it layer by layer for more than ninety minutes. He found a great deal he would have preferred not to have encountered, such as the remains of fifty servings of Tom Yam Goong from the adjacent Thai restaurant, but retrieved no trash of interest from the business.

Finally he climbed out of the first dumpster and climbed into the second. This turned out to be a more pleasant repository, as it contained only the leftovers of commercial transactions involving paper.

Cummings dug again. Though nothing was rotting, much was shredded. He stuck with his task, carefully looking through the streams of paper until he got near to the bottom. There he found several sheets of paper that had somehow missed the shredder in whole or in part. These were random parts of pages from three unrelated financial statements. He climbed out of the dumpster to take advantage of the brighter light of a street lamp.

Studying the fragments confirmed that they were evidence—not conclusive evidence, but at least encouragement. The numbers suggested that his assumptions were, or at least might be, correct.

He folded the sheets and put them in a pocket. He walked toward his car. He kept the windows open on the drive home, in a valiant but futile effort to dissipate the stench from his clothes.

Eighteen

The next morning, Cummings started the day searching the Internet for costume rental companies. He set his wristwatch timer and considered the relative merits of each. When the buzzer went off, he picked the one with the largest selection of costumes within five miles of his house.

"May I help you?" a young man, dressed as a comic book superhero, asked as Cummings walked in.

"Yes. I need a repairman's costume."

"What sort of repairman?"

"Any sort as long as one would commonly find such a person fixing something in a home, such as air conditioning or plumbing."

"Contemporary or historical?"

"Contemporary."

"Are you in a play?"

"No. I'm going to a costume party," Cummings lied.

"Honestly, being a repairman is a little boring. We have thousands of costumes here. Wouldn't you like something with more sparkle? Zorro? Sasquatch? Mary, Queen of Scots?"

"A repairman's costume will do fine."

"Okay, but you won't be winning any prizes with that!"

The clerk led Cummings to a dusty rack of men's service uniforms, dating from perhaps 1950 on. Cummings perused his options and chose a gray jumpsuit with a corporate logo,

Lefkowitz Appliances, stitched across the back and on the front of a matching cap.

"Do you rent props, too?" Cummings asked. "I'll need a tool kit."

"I'll look around."

"Good. Is there somewhere I can change into this?"

"You want to wear it out?"

"Yes. Why not?"

Cummings drove to Tom Daniels's neighborhood and parked. He picked up his toolkit from the passenger seat, straightened his cap and walked toward the house.

"I'm here to repair the washer," Cummings explained to Glenda, Tom's cleaning person, who answered the door.

"Mister Daniels isn't here. He went to the market."

"He said he wouldn't be in, but you would." Cummings knew this because Tom had remarked that he normally went out on Tuesdays to allow his cleaning person to do her job. "I'm from Lefkowitz Appliances. Mister Daniels called and asked us to come fix the washer."

"I guess you should come in then."

"Thank you. Can you show me where it is?"

Glenda brought him into the laundry room, which was located off the kitchen. On the way by the back door to the house, Cummings noticed two trash bags waiting to be taken out. They were tied with plastic closures.

Glenda returned to her work as Cummings pretended to inspect the washing machine. He waited fifteen minutes. When he heard the muffled sound of a vacuum cleaner start up in some distant part of the house, he called out:

"All fixed. I'll let myself out."

He went to the back door, picked up the trash bags and took them through the landscaped yard. Alleys run behind almost all Chicago residential streets. Cummings was safe in assuming that beyond the cedar fence marking the end of the property, he'd find one — as indeed he did.

He opened the back gate. Tom had a small detached garage, also a common feature in Chicago residential neighborhoods. Cummings crouched to one side of it, out of view of the house.

He opened the bags and began carefully digging through the contents. He found what he was looking for quickly, a welcome contrast to his earlier trash explorations. He put the items of interest into a pocket and resealed the bag.

As he did so, he heard the sound of a car entering the alley. He stood up and walked away casually from the garage.

It quickly became clear there were two cars, not one. In the first Cummings recognized Tom Daniels. A police car was behind him.

Cummings casually walked another hundred yards or so, then moved to the side and stood behind a tree. The cars passed him. Cummings was now slightly obscured and far enough away not to attract undue attention, yet he was still within visual and aural range.

He watched as Tom's garage door opened automatically and Tom drove in. The cruiser stopped, and two policemen got out. They ordered Tom out of his car.

"What is this about?" Tom asked, walking back into the alley.

"We're placing you under arrest for the murder of Therese Hickok," the first policeman said, brandishing a pair of handcuffs.

"You can't be serious," Tom protested.

"You have the right to remain silent. Anything you say may be used against you in a court of law ..." the policeman continued, pushing Tom against the side of his garage and cuffing him.

Cummings wasn't surprised. Indeed, he nodded his head in assent, wondering why the police hadn't made the arrest sooner. He continued his walk down the alley away from Tom's garage.

"Good afternoon, Rockland," Cummings said. He was speaking on his cell phone in his car, still parked down the street from Tom's home. "Is this a bad time to probe your remarkable mind?"

"I am not sure what would characterize a time as bad," Rockland responded. "If you are seeking to learn whether I'm in a coma or otherwise intellectually indisposed, the answer is no."

"I was just at Tom Daniels's house. He's been arrested for the murder of Therese Hickok."

"Is that a surprise?"

"I don't think so. He's been our prime suspect for some time. I became even more certain about him during the last few days. Anyway, I was digging through Tom's trash just before the police arrived. I found some printouts from the drug store — you know, the drug information they give you when you fill a prescription. Would you tell me what these drugs are used to treat?"

Cummings's next stop was Otto's house. Traffic was tangled, as it often is in Chicago, and it took him more than an hour to get there.

Mandrake did not open the door. Instead Cummings found himself greeted by an apparently distraught Otto. He was wearing sunglasses, and it was obvious that tears had been running down his face.

"What are you doing here?" Otto asked, not pleased to see Cummings.

"I want to speak to Mandrake."

"He's not here. He's gone."

"Gone where?"

"It's been a horrific day, and we've just heard dreadful news! Tom's been arrested for Therese's murder. He just called and asked me to get him a lawyer. Mandrake took off the moment he heard. He literally ran out of the house! How could you do this, you son of a bitch?" Otto exclaimed.

"How could I do what?" Cumming asked.

"Throw Tom to the wolves! What do you think I mean?"

"I didn't have anything to do with his arrest. May I come in?"

"I don't think so."

"Let him in," a voice behind Otto said. It was Sebastian. Otto didn't move.

"Let him in!" Sebastian insisted.

Otto moved away from the door, and Cummings walked into the entryway. Sebastian stood a few feet away, proportionately as unemotional as Otto was overwrought.

"We didn't have anything to do with this," Sebastian said.

"Anything to do with what?" Cummings asked.

"With any of this," Sebastian answered cautiously.

Cummings saw a shape in the corner of his eye. He glanced down the hallway. Barbara Cartland was lying on her side on the floor. She wasn't moving.

"Is something wrong with the dog?"

"She's dead," Sebastian said. "We don't know what happened. She just fell over. Possibly she had a heart condition."

At this Otto began to wail with the emotional fervor of a Norse berserker about to attack a medieval monastery. He fell to his knees, crawled to Barbara's lifeless body and keened over her remains.

"I imagine this is a difficult time for you," Cummings said, understating the obvious. "I came by just now to tell you Tom had been arrested, but you seem to know that already. I also wanted to give you some additional information. Perhaps it will be of some comfort."

"What information is that?" Sebastian asked.

"Tom is very ill. He has multidrug-resistant tuberculosis that doesn't appear to be responding to treatment. He's scared. He's not thinking clearly. I think he wanted the brooch because of its reputed health properties. I believe he tried to buy it from Therese, but she wouldn't sell it to him. So he decided to steal it by creating a diversion while she was speaking at the Mathers meeting. Of course, we know what happened — the diversion went out of control.

"From this point on I can only speculate. One of my theories is that Anunciación Hollingberry somehow figured out what had happened. Perhaps she's very low on funds. She may have blackmailed Tom with help from Mandrake. Does that seem possible to you?" Cumming asked, relishing this moment of cat and mouse.

"Yes, that's exactly what happened, isn't it, Otto?" Sebastian said.

"What do you mean?" Cummings asked.

"That's just what Mandrake told us," Sebastian explained. "Before he ran away. Isn't that right, Otto? Neither of us had any idea."

"Is that what Mandrake said? Did he also mention the furniture polish?"

"What furniture polish?"

"It was used as an accelerant. The brand name is Heirloom Formula. It was invented by Anunciación's husband. That's how she was able to identify it as the cause of the fire."

"I had no idea. Did Mandrake tell us that, Otto?"

"Leave me out of this," Otto wailed.

"I think you need to confirm my story, Otto," Sebastian said pointedly. "Otherwise, how is Cummings to know that we're telling him the truth?"

"Indeed, particularly as there are some inconsistencies," Cummings continued.

"What do you mean?" Sebastian asked.

"Anunciación just sold that furniture polish to an international conglomerate for an obscene amount of money, so it's unclear why she might want to blackmail Tom."

"But you just said ..."

"Yes, I did. Truthfully, I've already discarded that theory. I just wanted to see how you'd react. This leads me to my other theory, which seems to be the correct one. I spent some time in Boys Town the other night. I visited two of your bars, Sebastian. One has closed, and the other was practically empty. I also found several invoices from a liquor wholesaler in a trash bin behind your accountant's office. They were ninety days past due."

"That must have been an oversight."

"I have also searched *Crain's Chicago Business* for articles about your corporation. Apparently, you're involved in several condo projects that the paper described as stalled. The economy's taken such a toll on everyone, hasn't it?"

"Yes, it has, which makes my circumstances far from unusual. I still have substantial assets."

"Substantial is a relative term. Everyone has a budget and bills to pay. This is what I think happened: You and Otto saw Tom set the fire. Otto lied to the police in a misguided effort to protect Tom. That was understandable but foolish. Sebastian, you blackmailed Tom and told Otto that if he didn't cooperate, you'd make sure the police knew Tom had committed the crime and Otto had tried to conceal it. You also forced Mandrake to participate. You killed the dog in the last day or two. I'm basing that on the state of her rigor mortis. Of course, that was before you heard about Tom's arrest. That development might have led to a softer approach; but given that it's you, who's to say?"

"None of that's true," Sebastian insisted. "I love Otto."

"I think you find him colorful, and your marriage is good for business. As to love, poor Otto doesn't seem to have very good luck with men. Perhaps that's why he's a romance writer."

"It's true," Otto blurted out, turning to face Cummings. "Everything you just said is true. Sebastian told me there would be hell to pay if I tried to stop him from blackmailing Tom. That's why I told you I was the one being blackmailed and the brooch was missing. I thought if I sent you down the wrong road, perhaps you'd arrive at another solution that would keep Tom out of this mess."

"That was very silly," Cummings said.

"I didn't know what else to do!" Otto said, bursting into tears again. "I write about love. My strength is atmosphere, not plots!"

The front door opened. Cummings saw Mandrake rush in through the doorway. Behind him were several policemen.

The rivers of Middle Earth gushed down Mandrake's cheeks as he ran to Otto and embraced him.

"Ah thought he'd murdurr ye!" Mandrake cried out.

"I'm fine," Otto assured him, "just fine." Turning to Sebastian he said, "I realize we're about to be arrested, but I'm afraid there's no good time to tell you this. I'm divorcing you, Sebastian. You know as well as I that we haven't been happy for a long time. Mandrake and I have fallen in love. We plan to move to a nondenominational spiritual community outside of Fergus Falls."

"That be a toon in Minnesota," Mandrake added, passionately tightening his embrace around Otto's waist.

On the drive home Cummings had a sense that he'd overlooked something. After a few minutes he realized what it was—a small detail, perhaps something that would turn out to be nothing, but it needed to be looked into.

He walked into the living room, where Odin was sipping a cup of tea and reading the newspaper. He looked decidedly more cheerful.

"Tom Daniels has been arrested."

"Has he? So the case is closed?"

"Only part of the case. There's still the murder in Maine and how the two murders are connected."

"I think things are looking up at work," Odin said. "They're assigning me to a new project team. It tests sports equipment. If things go well, they said they'll hire me full-time as soon as next month."

"That's great, Odin. We'll celebrate when I get back. I'll take you to dinner wherever you like."

"Get back from where?"

"I need to make another trip to New England. Therese and Chess knew each other well. There must a connection between their murders. If not, it's the biggest coincidence in mortality since Thomas Jefferson and John Adams died on the same Fourth of July. I think the information I'm looking for may be in Boston."

"Boston?"

"Yes, where Tom and Otto went to college. I'll be gone for only a few days."

Nineteen

Cummings left early the next morning and stopped for the night at the edge of New York State. He starting driving again after breakfast and arrived at Ernestine's in midafternoon.

"Would you like some tea, dear?" Ernestine asked, even before he'd put his suitcases into one of the guest rooms. "I just asked Rebecca to fix a pot. Or would you prefer yours iced?"

"Either would be great, thank you," he responded.

Rebecca appeared from the kitchen.

"We seem to have run out of honey," she said to Ernestine. "Would you like sugar instead?"

"No, dear," Ernestine replied. "There's that jar I got from Chess last Christmas."

"Where did you put it?"

"It's in the pantry somewhere."

She returned to the kitchen. Ernestine patted the sofa cushion next to her, indicating that Cummings should sit close.

"So what are you doing back so soon?" Ernestine asked him. "Not that I'm not happy to see you."

Cummings explained that the Chicago case was all but solved, though Chess's murder seemed far from closure.

"Then you have to keep doing the investigating until there's an arrest," she insisted.

"I will, though I'd say that's more the police's job than mine."

"You know my estimation of our Officer Bernier," she said with a snort of Yankee contempt.

Cummings nodded in agreement as Rebecca came in with the tea. It came in a pot that matched Ernestine's tea cups on an antique silver tray with some cookies, lemon slices and the jar of honey. The label identified it as being from the Harpwater Hives.

"Do you have a relative named John?" Cummings asked Rebecca.

"Yes, dear. He's my son."

"I met him. I bought some of your candles. So this is your honey."

"Yes, dear. Chess Biederman was one of our best customers, may he rest in peace. You be sure to have some in your tea. It's wicked tasty!"

"I drink tea plain, but I'm sure it is."

Rebecca smiled and went back into the kitchen. Ernestine poured Cummings a cup and handed it to him. She poured one for herself, spooning a generous dollop of honey into her cup. She offered Cummings the cookies.

"Do you have any particular leads about Chess's murder?" she asked.

"Let's say I have a hunch," Cummings replied. "I think the solution may be in Boston."

The tea and cookies were refreshing, but they didn't truly relieve the fatigue of his long drive. Cummings excused himself. He took his suitcase into one of the guest rooms, kicked his shoes off and stretched out on the top of a chenille bedspread.

Some time later he was woken abruptly by a rough shake of his shoulder. It was Rebecca.

"Ernestine's been taken wicked sick," she said.

"What do you mean?" Cummings asked, not quite awake.

"I called for an ambulance. It's coming from Gethsemane now."

"Is she conscious?"

"She's been mumbling. I can't understand anything she is trying to say."

"Where is she?"

"On the floor in the parlor. She tried to get up off the sofa, and she fell."

Cummings ran to the front parlor. Ernestine, crumpled on her side with her legs askew, a puddle of vomit by her head, moaned almost inaudibly. Cummings knelt down and held her hand.

Rebecca offered to ride in the ambulance with Ernestine, but Cummings insisted he would go. He promised to phone Rebecca just as soon as there was news.

The emergency department at Gethsemane Hospital wasn't particularly busy, but there was still a considerable wait until a doctor emerged and spoke to Cummings.

"Are you allowed to talk to me?" Cummings asked, assuming there might be a problem with confidential health information.

"You're Mister Wanamaker, aren't you?"

"Yes."

"Mrs. Cutter identified you as her son-in-law."

This had been true, more or less. He and Terry certainly would have been married had this been legally available at the time. "So she's conscious?"

"She's lucid but experiencing severe abdominal pain, vomiting and diarrhea. It could be food poisoning. It could be the flu. It could be something else. We're running tests, and we're going to admit her. Do you happen to know what she's eaten today?"

"I don't know everything. I'm only visiting, and I arrived this afternoon. We had tea together. That included some shortbread that we both had, and I feel fine. I don't know what else she's had to eat today."

"We'll let you know when she's settled in her room."

"There was some honey," Cummings suddenly remembered. "She put honey into her tea. I drink mine plain."

"That's very unlikely to be the cause of the problem. Usually it's meat or poultry, sometimes dairy, sometimes fish."

"Right," Cummings said, "although I understand it's possible for honey to be naturally poisonous sometimes."

The doctor shrugged. "That might be possible, but I've never seen a case."

Cummings spent an hour with Ernestine in her room, then left. She was weak, nauseated and sliding in and out of wakefulness, but at least she didn't seem to be getting worse.

Cummings drove back to Horeb and immediately went into Ernestine's kitchen. He searched carefully, both in the refrigerator and the cupboards, hoping he might be able to identify the cause of the malady, assuming food was involved. There wasn't much food in the house, and what there was seemed fresh and properly stored.

Next he searched for the jar of honey. Curiously, he couldn't find it.

He suddenly remembered that he was supposed to call Rebecca but realized he didn't have her number, so he went into Ernestine's study. He searched her computer but didn't find an electronic address book. Next he looked in her drawers and eventually found a black leather personal directory. Fortunately, there was only one Rebecca listed, no surname or address. Cummings dialed the number, which he observed had a Samaria prefix. There was no answer. There was no voice mail.

Next he phoned Odin.

"Things aren't going well here. Ernestine is sick."

"How ill?"

"I think she'll be all right. It may just be the flu. I think I should stay a few extra days. I didn't really think about this until tonight, but I don't think she has anyone to help her. Terry was her only child. There are no nieces or nephews that I'm aware of."

"Of course. Do what you need to do."

"Thank you. I'll call you as soon as there's news. I love you."

"Tell her I hope she gets well soon," Odin said, although he and Ernestine had never actually met.

Finally Cummings phoned Rockland, who confirmed that Ernestine's symptoms might suggest a range of possible diagnoses of which the flu or food poisoning were the most likely. Cummings mentioned the honey. Rockland seemed tepid. "My money's on meat," he concluded.

The next morning Cummings returned to the hospital with a vase of wildflowers. Ernestine was improved enough to express appreciation and chat a bit, but she clearly still felt miserable.

"I know Rebecca's concerned about you," Cummings said, getting up to leave.

"She's late in the tide just like me," Ernestine said weakly.

Cummings wasn't sure what this expression meant. He thought it might be a metaphor for old age, but he didn't think this was the appropriate time to discuss Maine lingo.

"I tried to phone, but I couldn't reach her. I thought I'd drop by her home. She and John don't have an address listed. Do you know where she lives?"

"I've never been to her home. She lives with her son."

"Okay. Maybe I can reach him at the factory."

He tried to phone Rebecca again, but there was still no answer. He tried the Beiderman factory, but John wasn't in that day.

Cummings drove to Samaria. The farmers market wasn't operating, so he went to the crafts store. It was open, if empty, staffed by a young woman who was sitting on a stool in one corner reading a novel.

"Good morning," Cummings said. "Do you know John and Rebecca Harpwater?"

"Yes," she replied neutrally.

"Do you know where they live?"

"Why do you ask?" she asked, her neutrality changing key into suspicion.

"I'm Ernestine Cutter's son-in-law. Do you know Ernestine Cutter?"

"No."

"She lives in Horeb. Rebecca works for her. Ernestine's in the hospital. Rebecca will want to know how she is. I tried to call, but Rebecca's not answering her phone."

The woman thought about this, then said, "I'll get you the information," and disappeared into a back room.

While he was waiting, Cummings perused the crafts again. They were much the same as they had been the last, and only other, time he'd been in the shop.

The woman returned and handed Cummings a slip of paper.

He drove to the address. He wouldn't have found it without GPS. The house was off a main road, then off a side road, then at the end of a dirt road. It was worn and old, an eighteenth century saltbox that hadn't seen a coat of paint since at least the Reagan administration. The house seemed to be surrounded by some amount of land, mostly wooded, but it wasn't clear how many acres, as the boundaries weren't obvious. Certainly no neighbors, even distant ones, were visible when one looked through the surrounding trees. Cummings noticed that the trees were not particularly old. Apparently lumber was a source of income for this family.

Cummings walked around to the back door and banged on it. There was no response. He looked in the windows. The furnishings were modest but appeared comfortable. He saw no one, and no lights were on. Perhaps he had simply missed them last night, and they had both left early in the morning to go to work.

Cummings went back to his car and opened the glove compartment. There, among the assortment of items he always kept on hand, was a small pad of lined paper. He wrote a note, updating Rebecca about Ernestine's condition, and folded it.

He looked for the mailbox. It was not by the side of the road as one would expect in Maine, but he did locate it by the front door. He dropped the note in and headed back to the car.

His phone rang.

"Cummings? It's Rockland. What I'm about to tell you is highly speculative and most probably incorrect. After our last call, curiosity got the better of me. I did some research. Let's assume that your friend was poisoned with a substance that causes the symptoms you described. The degree of toxicity of whatever was used was likely only mild to moderate—after all, she's ill but not dead. Let's further assume the substance was widely available, easy to work with and relatively tasteless and odorless, all of which would contribute to the ease of poisoning. What about rhubarb leaves? The stalk, of course, is quite edible, but the leaves are poisonous."

"Rhubarb leaves," Cummings repeated, thinking about it.

"It's only a possibility, among other possibilities," Rockland reaffirmed. "As I said earlier, it's much more likely your friend has garden variety food poisoning, and the pun is unintentional."

"Thank you, Rockland."

Just for kicks, Cummings looked around for a garden. He didn't immediately see one. Scouting farther, he discovered a large area in a clearing in the woods fenced with high chain link. Inside, he saw a well-tended assortment of seasonal vegetables, including a verdant stand of rhubarb. Of course, this proved nothing: Rhubarb is as common as taciturnity in rural New England.

Ernestine's color was better when he went back to the hospital the next day, though she was still enervated.

"I'm feeling better," she insisted, but the untouched food on her lunch tray indicated that her appetite hadn't returned. "The doctor was in. He said they might let me go tomorrow or the next day."

"That's great! Did he say what's wrong with you?"

"I'm not sure they know for certain, dear."

"I have a question for you. I couldn't find the honey you ate yesterday."

"Why were you looking for that?"

"I thought it might be the source of your illness."

"It was right on the kitchen counter. Maybe Rebecca put it away."

"Is there any possibility Rebecca might have removed it from the house?"

"Cummings, I am absolutely positive that Rebecca has nothing to do with this. I have known the woman for years. Many years. Why would she want to harm me?"

"I didn't say that she does," Cummings responded.

The phone beside Ernestine's bed rang. It was Rebecca. She had received Cummings's note and was calling to see how Ernestine was getting on. They chatted for a few minutes, and then Ernestine said to Cummings, "She wants to thank you for leaving her the note."

"Please ask her about the honey."

"Rebecca, do you know what happened to that jar of honey I ate from the other day? I see. Hold on, dear." She covered the mouthpiece and told Cummings, "She accidentally broke the bottle while she was cleaning."

"So it's in the trash?"

"I imagine so, but today is trash day. More than likely, it's been picked up."

By the time Cummings brought Ernestine home from the hospital, which occurred two days later, she was more or less herself. He got her settled comfortably into her bed.

"Didn't you say something about going to Boston?" Ernestine asked.

"It can wait."

"I can look after myself for the afternoon. Now go!"

Cummings's first stop was the Cambridge office of the *Boston Basilisk*, the former underground weekly newspaper of radical leftist politics that presently existed only as an online vehicle for entertainment, sports banality and personal ads. The office was small, and the staff was sparse. Cummings had little trouble locating the editor. She introduced herself as Joyce.

"We take ads online only these days, but you can use that computer over there, if you'd like," she said politely, incorrectly anticipating Cummings's request.

"I'm not here about an ad. I'm wondering if you have a morgue."

"I don't think many of our readers are that erotically adventurous."

"I meant a newspaper morgue. Back issues."

"In the five years I've worked here, no one has ever asked to see a back issue."

"So you don't keep them?"

"Actually, we do. The owner insists. I think he secretly hopes that somehow we're going to return to the glory days when the *Basilisk* had actual content and supportive advertisers. We have every issue available in electronic form, dating back to the paper's founding in 1963."

"I'd like to look at a copy of the paper from 1985. Any average week will do."

"Okay. How about sometime in April?"

"That will be fine."

She led Cummings to an empty desk nearby, sat down at the computer and accessed some files.

"We date our editions on Sundays. How about April 7, 1985? Just use the cursor to go forward and backward."

She rose and returned to her desk.

Cummings carefully studied each page of the paper, looking for advertising from specialized retail shops. He found nine stores that might be of interest. An online check revealed that only two were still open. He noted their names and addresses.

Navigating through Boston has a justifiable reputation for complexity, and it took Cummings some time to find the first shop, even with GPS. This was Old Ways, advertised as "occult books and paraphernalia" in 1985. It was located in a strip mall in Somerville. The shop's name was prominent on a bright yellow plastic sign with a cornucopia, which also featured a tagline with a typographical error: "The New Age Horny of Plenty."

The proprietress was a thin woman in her early thirties with frizzy hair that hung down to the small of her back. She wore a floor-length red Victorian dress. She did not look up as Cummings entered.

"May I assist you?" she asked with marked tone of boredom.

"I'm just browsing," he responded. He spent a few minutes perusing the wares, the usual assortment of mundane objects of New Age cheerfulness, none of which were what he was looking for.

"You don't carry items for the more serious occult practitioner?"

"What do you mean?" she responded.

"Amulets and talismans, for example."

"I don't know what those are."

"Never mind. Thank you."

Cummings went on to the second venue, Pentacle Books. This was in the basement of a Victorian brownstone in Back Bay, which had become one of Boston's most fashionable shopping districts. Cummings assumed the shop predated the upscale surge, as it seemed unlikely that a bookstore of any sort could survive with the current retail rents in this neighborhood.

The interior was brick, and the light was inadequate. The walls were lined with bookshelves, crammed with books old and new, except for the far wall. A long glass display case stood in front of it with a cash register to one side. A small laptop lay near the register.

An elderly woman sat behind the display case. In dress and manner she looked professional but nondescript; she might have been behind the counter in any kind of business from a green grocer to a bank. She looked up at Cummings and nodded.

Cummings browsed for a few minutes. The books ranged from recent to rare. Cummings had no idea what knowledge they contained, but they all seemed priced for a tony retail location. The display case held a range of items: knives, bowls, objects carved with signs and sigils, and jewelry. It appeared to Cummings this shop was a much more likely venue for his purposes than the previous one.

"Have you worked here a long time?" Cummings asked.

"Yes," the woman responded. "I founded the shop in 1969."

"I'm a private investigator," Cummings responded. "I'm looking into two murders, one in Chicago and one in Maine. I'm trying to determine if there's a connection between them. I suspect the connection involves the fact that the killer of one, and someone else of importance, went to college together in Boston. Finally, I know that the killer has been collecting amulets and talismans since his undergraduate days."

"Do you have some identification, Mister ...?"

"Wanamaker. I'm afraid I've run out of business cards. Here's my driver's license."

He showed it to her. She looked at it carefully.

"I can assure you I'm not going to ask you anything sensitive," Cummings said reassuringly.

"What do you want to know?" she replied.

"Do you recall any customers named Tom Daniels or Jules Verne? Oddly, that's his real name. He goes by Tom Daniels, at least these days. He would have lived in Boston in the 1980s."

"It sounds familiar, but I can't place it."

"What about Anunciación Hollingberry?"

"No."

"Otto Verissimo?"

"No."

"Do you know of an object called the Craddock Brooch?"

"Actually I do. I sold it some years ago. When I get in better quality occult books or objects, and they don't sell here within a few months, I sell at auction."

"Do you use Clarkson's Auction House in Chicago?"

"Yes. It's one of the auctioneers I use. I sold some pieces there a few weeks ago. They belonged to Emma Hardinge Britten. There was a scrying dish and a lingam, I believe."

"Would you be willing to verify if your vendor number was CB788?"

"I don't think I'd feel comfortable with that. I'm sorry."

"I understand. Thank you for your time."

Cummings turned to leave when the woman asked, "Did you say you're investigating a murder in Maine? Where in Maine? I have a summer house there."

"Horeb."

"Really? My house is in Gethsemane. That's not ten miles away. Who was murdered?"

"A man named Chess Biederman. Did you know him?"

"I don't believe so. But I do know someone in Horeb, a woman named Elektra Philemon. She used to clean for me."

"I know her well."

"Do you? What a coincidence! She used to clean my house and the shop here. She lived in Boston at the time, of course. This would have been, let's see, the mid-1970s. The customers thought she was fun, so sometimes she also helped out in the shop."

"Did she? She is effervescent."

"That she is! What was that name you mentioned? Daniel something ..."

"Tom Daniels."

"Elektra moved to Maine, and we lost touch. I did hear from her some years ago. She asked my advice about financing a restaurant. She was hoping to open a Greek taverna somewhere. I don't know the first thing about restaurants, so I wasn't much help. I didn't hear from her after that for a long time — well, except for Christmas cards — but she did phone me a few months ago."

"Did she?"

"Yes. She asked about an old customer, if I had a current address."

"And was that, by any chance, Tom Daniels?"

"My memory isn't what it once was, and I have thousands of customers. I'm almost sure she asked about Daniel somebody. I recall that I did look up the name in my client records. I gave her whatever information I had."

"Would you mind checking your records for Tom Daniels?"

"Certainly. I have a database. It will just take a moment." She opened the laptop and soon had the information.

"Yes. We do have a Tom Daniels with a Chicago address. His last transaction was two years ago. I sold him an amulet. Is that the man you're referring to?"

"Yes."

"Has he been killed?"

"I'm afraid he's been arrested for murder."
"Oh, my!"

Deuteronomy Smelt was immersed in thought. He'd been
sitting in his room all afternoon, thinking, and he wasn't
arriving at meaningful conclusions.

He glanced at his desk and noticed that the bushy beard
he'd worn on his ill-conceived trip to Zion hadn't been put
away. At that moment a trip to the attic seemed to be a good
distraction from his growing irritation with himself.

In the attic Deuteronomy located the appropriate storage
box and carefully replaced the beard.

On his way back his eye caught something unexpected. It
startled him.

He returned to his room and made a call.

"Ernestine, this is Deuteronomy. How are you?"

"I'm improving, thank you for asking."

"I didn't realize you'd been ill. Are you alone there? Do
you need anything?"

"No, no. I have my housekeeper, and Cummings is
visiting."

"I was hoping he was. May I speak to him?"

"He's in Boston just now, but he should be back by
evening."

"Thank you, Ernestine. I'm going to drop off a message
for Cummings. Now you let me know if you need anything."

He scrawled out a message on a postcard, this one with a
black-and-white photo of a globe with a banner: "Greetings
from the 1937 World's Fair." The message read, "My
deductions may have been incorrect. Please come see me as
soon as possible."

He put on a tie and sports jacket and left the house for the brief walk to Ernestine's. So as not to disturb her, he slid the card under her door.

Twenty

Cummings arrived back at Ernestine's late in the afternoon. Ernestine mentioned Deuteronomy's postcard. Cummings read it.

"Maybe I should go over there," Cummings said. "Have you had dinner?"

"I am just fine. Go and see Deuty."

"One question. Could you tell me about the honey Chess gave you? When did he give it to you?"

"It must have been at my annual holiday party. He probably brought it as a hostess gift. You are developing an obsession with that honey!"

"One last thing. Was Elektra at your holiday party?"

"Of course, dear. You remember my Christmas parties — I invite just about everybody in the village!"

Cummings rang Deuty's buzzer, and Elektra opened the door.

"Mister Deuty say you go into his room when you arrive," she said, leading him to Deuty's door. She pounded on it. "Mister Cummings he come in."

"Very well. Thank you, Elektra."

Deuteronomy looked agitated. Cummings didn't probe. Deuteronomy Smelt wasn't the sort of man who would appreciate that.

"Thank you for coming so promptly," Deuteronomy said. "Truthfully, you are here earlier than I'd hoped. I've invited some people for coffee and dessert."

"Who?"

"Rebecca Harpwater and her son."

"Why?"

"I believe there are some questions that need to be asked. I've been rethinking what we know about Chess's murder. I fear I've misinterpreted the facts."

"In what way?"

"The key thing is that we need to allow for a wider range of solutions. I don't think it's prudent to talk more now. Elektra knows I've invited Rebecca and John, which she thinks is curious. I don't want to add to her concerns by making it appear that you and I are engaged in skullduggery. She and Rebecca are good friends, you know. Very good friends."

"No, I didn't."

"Can you come back at 7:30?"

"Certainly."

"Thank you. Perhaps you'll be good enough to follow my lead tonight."

"Of course. However, I've just come from Boston, where I learned something I think I should tell you."

Just then Elektra knocked on the door to announce she'd just made some muffins.

"You'll have to tell me later," Deuteronomy replied.

When Cummings returned a few minutes after the appointed time, Deuteronomy was making small talk in the parlor with Rebecca and John Harpwater. All of them seemed ill at ease. Cummings wondered if this was due to the social hierarchy in Maine, in which the classes coexist but rarely coalesce, or if Rebecca and John were simply feeling put on the spot.

Elektra had prepared a delectable assortment of Mediterranean pastries arranged attractively on doilies on a silver tray. She poured and distributed cups of coffee, then left the room.

"It was wicked kind of you to take care of Ernestine," Rebecca said to Cummings. "I know she appreciates it."

"I'm happy to help," Cummings said.

"My mother always said, 'what's the good of having neighbors if you can't help them when they need it?' I don't know that the young people think like that anymore."

"I'm not certain if they do or they don't," Deuteronomy said. "My granddaughter wants to go to medical school and then be a doctor in Africa, but I know lots of young people who don't see past their own noses. But I think I know what you mean. Years ago things made a lot more sense than they do today. For example, Chess's murder. That doesn't make any sense at all."

"That is the truth!" Rebecca agreed.

"My friend Cummings and I have been trying to determine what happened."

"Are you working with the County Sheriff?" John asked.

"No. This is more informal," Deuteronomy explained. "That's why I've invited you both tonight. We thought you might be able to help us."

"How?" Rebecca responded, surprised.

"You knew Chess, of course. And John, you worked for him. I also understand you were personal friends."

"That's true."

"Do you know of anything unusual around the time Chess was killed, John? Perhaps something you haven't told the police."

"No, I don't believe so," John replied.

"You're sure? You're really sure?" Deuteronomy probed. "I've been told you played poker with Chess the night before he disappeared."

"That's true. It wasn't just the two of us, of course. It takes four to play poker," John responded, sounding defensive.

"Perhaps I could ask Rebecca a question," Cummings interjected.

Deuteronomy shot him a look of disapproval for changing the subject. Cummings continued anyway.

"Is there any more of the honey that Ernestine ate the day she became ill?" he asked Rebecca.

"I am wicked sorry about that! I accidentally broke the bottle, and I put it in the trash."

"I know. Ernestine told me. Were there any other bottles? I mean at her house?"

"No. There was just the one. I'd given her a few bottles of honey myself, but those were used up already. Do you think that's what made Ernestine sick?"

"We wouldn't know unless we tested that particular bottle, and that doesn't seem possible now."

"I'm just glad she's all right," Rebecca said.

"We all are," Deuteronomy said. "John, perhaps we could talk about that poker game."

"Excuse me," Cummings said, rising and walking in the direction of the downstairs bathroom used by guests. John began to describe what he remembered about the poker game. Deuteronomy shot Cummings another look as he left the room.

The bathroom was on the other side of the house, near the kitchen and down the hall from what Cummings had always assumed was Elektra's room. All three rooms were accessed from the same hallway.

Cummings stood and listened. He heard a sitcom laugh track coming from inside Elektra's room. This suggested she had gone off duty or was at least taking a break.

Cummings walked into the kitchen and quietly closed the door behind him. He noticed several doors in one wall. He opened the first. It was a broom closet. He opened the next. It was a rather large pantry.

He turned on the light and went inside, quickly perusing the shelves. Soon he found what he was looking for: five jars of Harpwater Hives honey, identical to the one he'd seen Ernestine use. He turned off the light and returned to the living room.

"As I remember I lost about twenty dollars, and Chess won about twenty dollars," John told Deuteronomy, winding up his account of the poker game. Cummings sat down. "I think the others broke even. We all had to work the next day, so we broke up early, about ten o'clock."

"Where did you go after that?"

"Home, of course," John responded, surprised by the question. "Where else would I go?"

Elektra appeared and checked on the coffee.

"Anyone want more coffee?" she asked.

"I certainly don't," John replied. "I'll be up all right."

"You do make strong coffee, Elektra," Rebecca said with a smile.

"Is the Greek way," Elektra said.

"You really ought to open up that restaurant in Portland," Cummings said cheerfully. "Your pastries are excellent."

Elektra smiled.

"It's a real shame," Rebecca said. "I know she's tried everything. The banks won't give her a loan because they say restaurants are too risky. Ernestine, bless her heart, said she'd put up some of the money, but Elektra couldn't raise the rest. Isn't that right?"

"Is right," Elektra said, "but hope I never give up."

"What about Chess? Did you ask him?" Cummings asked in a casual tone.

"No. I barely knows the Chess."

"Elektra, I think you've forgotten," Rebecca reminded her. "You did ask him. He wouldn't give it to you. Remember? He said he talked to some adviser who told him restaurants mostly all lost money."

"Yes. I forget," Elektra nodded. She picked up the coffee pot and went back to the kitchen.

Cummings observed that Deuteronomy's expression had changed from irritation to intrigue. He seemed like someone who wasn't sure he wanted to go on a trip just then but was willing to wait and see if the weather was agreeable when he got off the plane.

Cummings turned to Rebecca and John.

"Tell me, do you sell gift baskets during the holidays?"

"Yes," John said, "we started a few years ago. We put in our honey and maple candy and candles and beeswax hand lotion."

"You do label the honey in your gift baskets?"

"Of course! It's also on the cellophane wrapping around the basket. We don't want people to forget where the goodies came from."

"Who bought these gift baskets last year? Individuals? Businesses? About how many did you sell?"

"Oh, we made a lot of them, more than one hundred fifty."

"Chess bought a lot, may he rest in peace," Rebecca said.

"He did," John said. "He said he wanted to support our business, so he ordered forty baskets. He gave them out to employees and friends as holiday gifts."

"That was our biggest order," Rebecca said. "We were very grateful."

"We were. We made him a big thank you gift basket. Do you remember that, Mother?"

"I do," Rebecca replied.

"And what was in Chess's gift basket?"

"The same as everyone else's but more of everything, and there was also a holiday card."

"By any chance did Elektra help you make up these gift baskets?" Cummings asked.

"Elektra?" Deuteronomy repeated, surprised.

"Yes. Yes, she did. She was a big help to us," Rebecca said.

"We were just overwhelmed last year," John explained. "Elektra came to our home the day after Thanksgiving and stayed all weekend, helping us make up the baskets. Then she helped me deliver the local orders and get the others to the post office. We couldn't have done it without her."

"When you say Elektra helped you deliver the orders," Cummings continued, "do you mean that you delivered some, and she delivered some?"

"Yes," John replied.

"Do you remember who delivered Chess's order?"

"Elektra did. I remember, because I knew there'd be guys at the factory to unload all those baskets. I sent her there while I did the run to the post office."

"Oh, my," Deuteronomy said suddenly. Cummings looked at him. Deuteronomy appeared to be quite glum.

"Are you feeling poorly?" Rebecca asked.

"How very disturbing!" Deuteronomy said. "It seems I correctly understood that I was going against the wind, but I continued to move the rudder in another wrong direction. Would you please excuse me for a moment?"

He rose and went up the stairs.

"Do you need anything?" Rebecca called after him, but he didn't respond. She turned to Cummings. "I hope he's all right. Elektra says he's been acting odd all day."

Elektra reappeared.

"Anyone want more glyka?" she said, indicating the dessert tray.

"I'm stuffed!" Rebecca said. "They were delicious, Elektra."

"Wicked tasty," John agreed.

Deuteronomy reappeared on the stairs, heading back to the parlor. He was carrying a red plastic canister.

"I found this in the attic earlier today. I thought perhaps it was John's and that Elektra was hiding it," Deuteronomy announced.

"No. It's not mine," John said.

"I realize that now," Deuteronomy continued. "It appears this canister has been rinsed carefully but it still has a vague odor of gasoline."

"Why is that important?" John asked.

"This from the boat," Elektra said. "We use this on boat if we are out of the gas."

"The canister we keep for the boat is blue, and we store it on the boat," Deuteronomy replied. "I'm afraid, Elektra, this held the accelerant you used to burn down the Ephemera Museum."

"You think I do this?" Elektra scoffed. "Why I does this? I quiet Greek housekeeper, not Medea!"

"I think I can explain your motive. It was a diversion," Cummings explained. He glanced at Rebecca and John. They both looked shocked.

"Yes," Deuteronomy agreed. "I concocted the absurd notion that Chess was assassinated to tie up a loose end from the Cold War, and you took it up as a way to divert attention from what was really going on. What a fool I was! No wonder I can't write books that anyone wants to read anymore. Worse, I thought that John here ... well, it doesn't matter now. John, you must accept my apologies."

"You think I killed Chess?" John asked, startled.

"No. No, I don't. I was mistaken," Deuteronomy confessed.

"Don't be hard on yourself," Cummings said to Deuteronomy. "Your suppositions were clever; they just weren't correct. The truth is Elektra killed Chess because he wouldn't finance her restaurant."

"You must be mistaken," Rebecca stammered.

"I do no such thing!" Elektra insisted.

"Revenge is important to you. You told me so. I don't think you meant to kill him, just to make him sick. You made a toxic botanical extract, perhaps from rhubarb leaves, and put it into Chess's thank you gift basket," Cummings continued. "What you didn't know was that Chess was allergic to honey."

"How did you learn that?" Deuteronomy marveled.

"Because you told me that Chess was allergic to many things, and he gave Ernestine a bottle of honey as a hostess gift." Cummings turned to Elektra. "You may not have known he was allergic to honey, but you were at that party, and you saw him give Ernestine the jar. You realized he might give away all the honey you'd poisoned."

"You think I carry bottles of the poison in the handbag of me?" Elektra demanded.

"No. I think you're very selective. You did your best to retrieve as many bottles of that poisoned honey as you could from the people Chess gave it to. That's likely why there are five jars of honey in your pantry now. But I guess you weren't able to get the bottle back from Ernestine," Cummings replied.

"Anyway, you changed your plan. You made another batch of poison, probably delivered in something you cooked, which Chess ate when he visited Deuteronomy.

"At this point I don't know exactly what happened. Did you inadvertently make the poison too strong? Did Chess go into anaphylactic shock due to an allergy to a compound you used? My guess is that Chess collapsed immediately after leaving from a visit with Deuteronomy and fell somewhere between the door and his car. Deuteronomy likely retreated to his room immediately after Chess's departure, so he didn't notice. In any case Chess died, and somehow you moved him, probably in that large wheelbarrow you keep in the garden. It was dark. You wheeled Chess to the boat, which was parked far enough from Ernestine's house that she didn't see or hear you.

"Ernestine was having septic work done. The workmen had left a small excavator for the duration. You used it to load Chess into the boat and push his body into the front cabin. That explains the scratches on the side of the boat.

"The next day you had the guys from the shipyard come by and shrink-wrap the boat. You had to hurry in case the body started to smell before it froze. Once the boat was wrapped, you knew there was almost no chance the body would be discovered until late spring, and by then it would likely have eroded to such an extent that the murder couldn't be traced back to you."

"This is nonsense! How I know do this?"

"Because you're an avid reader, and you've read all of my books," Deuteronomy proposed. "I used poisoned honey as a plot device in *Martinis Are My Business,* although my character only became ill from it. The body in the boat came from *Cat and Spouse*."

"This is lies, all this lies!" Elektra shrieked.

"There's more," Cummings said. "I suspected there was a connection between Chess's death and that of his ex-wife, Therese Hickok."

"That's right. I'd forgotten Chess and Therese were married," Rebecca said.

"Yes," Cummings said, "but they remained friends. In fact, Chess used to ask Therese for business advice. Therese was the person who told Chess not to invest in your restaurant, Elektra, which he must have told you. You were furious. You found out that Therese was living in Chicago. You phoned someone you knew there, someone you'd met working in an occult store in Boston. At this point there was some serendipity. It turned out Tom knew Therese. They were both members of the same occult society."

"You think I kill Therese? How I do this?" Elektra protested.

"I don't think you killed Therese. What you did do was encourage Tom Daniels to scare her but good. Tom's very ill and in a terrible mental state. He mentioned the Craddock Brooch. You probably had never heard of it, but it didn't matter. You knew amulets and talismans fascinated him because you used to sell them to him. You encouraged his belief in the brooch's healing properties. You suggested he steal the brooch from Therese; it would be easy if he created a diversion. You suggested spontaneous combustion. Deuteronomy, I assume that's also in one of your books?"

"Yes, it is. It's in *Vodka Is My Passion*. That was the sequel to *Martinis Are My Business*. Sales were unexpectedly good for the first book, so my publisher asked for a sequel.

The second book didn't sell as well. Apparently my readership sobered up over the years."

"And what was the result of the spontaneous combustion in your novel?"

"It was a diversion. The fire was put out before it caused any real harm."

"So that's it," Cummings concluded. "The fire went out of control."

"Bravo!" Deuteronomy said.

John and Rebecca looked horrified.

"I not mean to kill," Elektra said, wailing pitifully as she sank to her knees. "Is *tragoidia! Tragoidia!* This the fates do! I play the pranks, but the fates make go all wrong! Is not my fault!" She beat the floor with her fists.

"I fear one of us should phone the police," Deuteronomy suggested sadly.

Later, after Elektra had been led away in handcuffs and the Harpwaters retreated, with Rebecca in tears and John looking ashen, Deuteronomy offered Cummings a brandy. Cummings declined, but Deuteronomy poured himself one and sank into the sofa.

"How could she do such terrible things?" he asked plaintively.

"I can't say," Cummings answered. "Sadly, we can define what people do but I don't think we can really understand it. Human behavior just doesn't make sense. Amoebas behave rationally. People do not."

Twenty-One

Six weeks later a second article about Cummings appeared in the *Chicago Tribune,* this one lauding him for helping the police solve the murder of Therese Hickok. This resulted in another series of oddball calls from prospective clients, as well as a polite but firm email from a Chicago Police Department media outreach person. He informed Cummings that he was to receive a civilian commendation and politely suggested that Cummings would best serve the cause of justice by staying out of police business.

The Maine police did not acknowledge Cummings's contribution, but curiously, Mandrake did. As best as Cummings could tell, Mandrake felt that Cummings had played a role in creating the conditions for his romance with Otto, and for this Mandrake was grateful. He stayed in touch.

Mandrake and Otto struck a deal with the District Attorney. They were granted immunity from prosecution in exchange for testifying against Tom and Sebastian. Both were prepared to toss Sebastian to any available carnivores, but testifying against Tom was painful. Ultimately they felt the circumstances left them little choice, and so they agreed.

The last time Cummings heard from Mandrake, he and Otto had moved to Minnesota. They were accessible only by email and a post office box. A winter wedding was anticipated after Otto's divorce from Sebastian was finalized. Otto was working on a new book, set just prior to the Russian Revolution. The working title was *The Menshevik Caress.*

In Maine Elektra was awaiting trial. Deuteronomy mourned the loss of Elektra and had turned to Ernestine for support. Although she hadn't said as much, Cummings suspected something romantic might be brewing between them.

Deuteronomy began to write again. He asked Cummings for his permission to use him as a character in a true crime novel about Chess's and Therese's murders. The title was *To Hive and Hive Not.*

A few months later Deuteronomy sent Cummings a draft. Cummings eagerly turned to the first page.

Chapter One

"Where's the body, Bob?" Detective Wanamaker asked, shaking the rain from his L.L. Bean raincoat. It was a cold, drizzly morning in early June, the kind you sometimes get in Maine when spring doesn't end, and summer doesn't come.

"In the boat," Officer Robert Bernier answered. Bob was a man who knew everything and said nothing — the kind of man you could trust.

"How'd the victim get it?" Cummings asked. He pulled back the plastic covering that had wrapped the sailboat during the winter and studied the corpse within. Sure enough, it was a dead body. Its shriveled and desiccated state suggested it had been there a long time.

"We'll have to wait for the coroner on that," Bob said, "but the body's in bad shape. Truthfully, we might never know what happened."

Cummings nodded. It was going to be that kind of murder.

Meet Author David Steven Rappoport

David Steven Rappoport is the author of two plays produced Off-Broadway, *Cave Life* and *The Upper Depths,* and has also written for radio and television.

His short story, "Leftovers," was a winner of the Mystery Times 2015 competition and is featured in an anthology of winning stories from Buddhapuss Ink.

He is a graduate of the Master of Fine Arts: Creative Writing Program at Goddard College. He currently lives in Chicago.

David's website is www.davidstevenrappoport.com.

CPSIA information can be obtained at www.ICGtesting.com
Printed in the USA
BVOW08s2359090416

443197BV00002B/4/P